LOVE INS

INSPIRATIONAL ROMANCE

True love always
finds a way...

The Amish Widow's
Christmas Hope

CARRIE LIGHTE

TRUE LARGE PRINT

"I'm not giving Eleanor a ride home. Why would you think I was?"

"Because she told me you were."

Walker shook his head. "*Neh*. That's not the truth."

Fern bristled. "Are you saying I'm not telling the truth about Eleanor telling me that or Eleanor's not telling the truth about you telling her that?"

"I'm saying I never had any plans to give Eleanor a ride home, so someone is mistaken." Walker crossed his arms against his chest. "And it isn't me."

"Well, my ears work fine, so I'm not the one who's mistaken, either," Fern retorted. "I guess that means Eleanor must have dreamed it all up! Just like she must have imagined you're her suitor."

Walker faltered backward, dropping his arms to his sides. "I never said I'd take her home. And I'm certainly not courting her—or anyone else, for that matter. She must have gotten the wrong impression."

"Just like I must have gotten the wrong impression about how you felt about me?"

Carrie Lighte lives in Massachusetts next door to a Mennonite farming family, and she frequently spots deer, foxes, fisher cats, coyotes and turkeys in her backyard. Having enjoyed traveling to several Amish communities in the eastern United States, she looks forward to visiting settlements in the western states and in Canada. When she's not reading, writing or researching, Carrie likes to hike, kayak, bake and play word games.

Books by Carrie Lighte

Love Inspired

Amish of Serenity Ridge

Courting the Amish Nanny
The Amish Nurse's Suitor
Her Amish Suitor's Secret
The Amish Widow's Christmas Hope

Amish Country Courtships

Amish Triplets for Christmas
Anna's Forgotten Fiancé
An Amish Holiday Wedding
Minding the Amish Baby
Her New Amish Family
Her Amish Holiday Suitor

Visit the Author Profile page
at Harlequin.com for more titles.

The Amish Widow's Christmas Hope

Carrie Lighte

LOVE INSPIRED

INSPIRATIONAL ROMANCE

LOVE INSPIRED®

INSPIRATIONAL ROMANCE

Recycling programs
for this product may
not exist in your area.

ISBN-13: 978-1-335-42972-8

The Amish Widow's Christmas Hope

Copyright © 2020 by Carrie Lighte

This edition published by arrangement with Harlequin Books S.A.

For questions and comments about the quality of this book, please contact us at CustomerService@Harlequin.com.

Love Inspired
22 Adelaide St. West, 40th Floor
Toronto, Ontario M5H 4E3, Canada
www.Harlequin.com

Printed in U.S.A.

And, lo, the angel of the Lord came upon them,
and the glory of the Lord shone round about
them: and they were sore afraid. And the angel
said unto them, Fear not: for, behold, I bring you
good tidings of great joy, which shall be to all
people. For unto you is born this day in the city
of David a Saviour, which is Christ the Lord.
—*Luke* 2:9–11

And the Word was made flesh,
and dwelt among us, (and we beheld his glory,
the glory as of the only begotten of the Father,)
full of grace and truth.
—*John* 1:14

For my mother,
who reads my books first and fastest

Chapter One

Fern Glick crouched down so her face was level with her children's faces. "I should be home by lunchtime. Remember to use your best manners and do whatever Jaala asks you to do," she instructed them.

Patience, five, nodded obediently, but Phillip was distracted by the chatter of Jaala's grandchildren as they put on their coats and boots in the mudroom at the opposite end of the kitchen.

"Can we go outside, too, *Mamm*?" the six-year-old asked.

"*Jah*, of course you may. Be sure to button your coats to the top buttons—it's chilly out there," Fern answered. Rising, she kissed the tops of their heads before the pair raced to the mudroom. Fern smiled when she heard the other children welcome them enthusiastically.

"The *kinner* sound like they're already having *schpass* and they haven't gotten out the door yet," Jaala said as she entered the kitchen and took the broom from its hook. "Didn't I tell you the more the merrier?"

"That's true for *kinner*, but not necessarily for *eldre*. Especially when it means there aren't enough beds to go around. I feel *baremlich* about imposing on you like this when you already have company here for *Grischtdaag*."

"They're not company—they're *familye*," Jaala said with a wave of her hand. "You and the *kinner* don't have to leave on the twenty-third—you're *wilkom* to stay here and celebrate *Grischtdaag* with us."

Despite Jaala's warm hospitality, Fern couldn't wait to leave Serenity Ridge,

Maine. The only reason she was staying until the following Saturday was because that's when she could secure the most affordable transportation home. If it was up to her, she wouldn't have returned to Maine in the first place.

Earlier in the month, she'd been contacted by an attorney regarding her recently deceased uncle Roman's estate. The attorney said Fern was to receive an inheritance, but he couldn't provide additional details until she met with him in person. Which meant Fern and her children had to journey nearly one thousand miles from their home in Geauga County, Ohio.

Fern had arranged to stay with Jaala and her husband, Abram, the district's deacon, but Jaala hadn't known her two sons and their families would be visiting at the same time—they weren't supposed to arrive for another week. The Amish had a knack for making room for everyone, but Jaala and Abram's modest house was stretched to the limit.

Jaala was the only person Fern had kept in touch with since she left Serenity Ridge eight years ago, so it didn't seem right to call on anyone else for lodging. Getting a room at a local inn was also out of the question: Fern spent every cent of the meager savings she'd managed to scrape together on transportation to Maine.

"Roman must have bequeathed you something substantial," Jaala speculated as she bent to sweep crumbs into the dust bin. "Otherwise, whatever he left you could have been shipped to Ohio."

Fern couldn't imagine her uncle leaving her anything of significant value. While it was true she'd helped her cousin Gloria care for him for over a year while he was recovering from a stroke and then she'd lived with them for two more years after that, Fern had rarely communicated with Roman since she left Maine. She never visited, either. In fact, she'd even missed Gloria's funeral five years ago because she'd just given birth to Patience and couldn't travel with a newborn. And Fern hadn't been able to leave Ohio to attend Roman's funeral this past November, either, since she was tending to her cousin's wife, who was on bed rest during the last month of her pregnancy.

"I assume he gave the *haus* and any savings he had to Gloria's daughter because she's Roman's closest living relative," Fern suggested. She supposed it was greedy, but once or twice she caught herself hoping whatever Roman left her, it was something that could be sold quickly so she could use the money to compensate for the expense of their trip.

"But Jane's only seven," Jaala commented. "If Roman left the *haus* to her, Walker will either have to manage the property or sell it and put the money in a trust fund for her until she's of age."

Fern turned her back and rinsed a couple stray coffee cups in the sink so Jaala couldn't read her expression. Walker Huyard, Jane's father, had been the love of Fern's life. Or so she believed during the two and a half years they'd secretly courted when Fern lived in Serenity Ridge. The couple had planned to get married the autumn they turned twenty-one, but that September, Fern was called back to Ohio to care for her ailing aunt.

Initially, Fern thought she'd return to Maine in time for wedding season, but when it was clear she'd be delayed indefinitely, they both pledged to wait however long they had to in order to become husband and wife. Yet Fern had barely been away for two months when she learned Walker had wed Gloria instead. Jane was born the following summer.

Fern wasn't merely hurt, angry and disappointed; she was in shock. Barely able to eat, sleep, pray or speak for weeks on end, it was as if she were in mourning for someone who'd died a sudden and unexpected death. She was just beginning to recover physically and emotionally when the aunt she'd been caring for passed away and her aunt's house was repossessed by the bank, leaving Fern homeless. It was desperation, not love, that had caused Fern to marry Marshall, a widower twelve years her senior. More accurately, it was *resignation*; Fern had given up believing there *was* such a thing as true love.

But in Marshall she'd found a man who, although not outwardly affectionate or expressive, was kind and considerate and until he fell ill, he'd given her a house and stability. In turn, she did her best to offer him companionship and care. The unspoken truth between them was that he'd married her out of loneliness and she'd married him out of poverty. Over time, their fondness for each other deepened and although Fern never felt toward Marshall the way she once felt toward Walker, she didn't regret marrying him. How could she, when he'd fathered their two beloved children? *Besides, Marshall never hurt me the way Walker did...*

"Ouch!" Fern yelped as the water

scalded her fingers, snapping her back to the present.

"Are you all right, dear?" Jaala asked.

"I'm fine. I'd better get going—it's almost nine o'clock."

Fern bundled into her coat and covered her prayer *kapp* with her best winter church bonnet, then stepped outside. It was only the fifteenth of December, but Jaala mentioned that two days before, a heavy rain had frozen over, coating everything with ice. It had since melted, but this morning the air smelled of impending snow. Fern glanced across the dirt driveway toward the barn, where the children were straddling the fence, pretending they were riding horses.

As Phillip bounced up and down, Fern visually assessed the railing and determined it wouldn't give way beneath his weight. He was such a sturdy child, built like his father. He had his father's dark hair and eyes, too. But Marshall's demeanor was so understated he seemed detached, whereas Phillip couldn't contain his exuberance for life and his affection for people.

Patience, on the other hand, was a diminutive replica of her mother—fair-haired, fair-skinned, freckled and petite—but Fern hoped that's where the similarities ended. *Waifish* was the word someone once used to describe Fern as a girl and she didn't want her daughter to grow up feeling like a ragamuffin, too.

Gott *willing, maybe I can get a full-time job at Weaver's Fabric Shop and I'll be allowed to bring the* kinner *to work until they're old enough to start* schul. *Then I might be able to afford to rent a place of our own*, Fern schemed.

Shortly after Fern's husband died two years earlier, she'd had to sell their house—at a loss—because she couldn't keep up with the mortgage payments. Fern and the children moved in with Fern's cousin on her mother's side, Adam, and his wife, Linda, and their children. Fern contributed what she could to the family's expenses and she helped mind their brood, too. She'd even given up her part-time job so she could manage the household while Linda was on bed rest during her fifth pregnancy. However, in spite of Fern's helpfulness, the couple had been strongly hinting it was time for her and the children to find another place to live.

Having lost both of her parents when she was still a baby, Fern was accustomed to being shifted from one relative's home to another. Whenever someone in her extended family needed an extra person to work on a farm, mind children or tend to an infirmed elder, Fern would pack up her suitcase and go stay with them until her help was needed elsewhere. It wasn't that she didn't want to be of service to her extended family members, nor was it that anyone was unkind to her. But Fern had grown up longing for a permanent place to call home.

I'm twenty-nine and not much has

changed, she reflected. *I still want a permanent place to call home...but now I want it more for my* kinner *than for myself.*

Patience's waving from across the driveway snapped Fern out of her daze. She giggled; the child had misbuttoned her coat, but at least it was fastened to the top. Fern lifted her gloved hand to wave back and then started down the lane.

Walker climbed into his buggy, hoping the meeting with the attorney wouldn't take long; this was a busy week at work. During the warmer months, he was employed full-time by an *Englisch* tree service, but in winter, he took odd jobs here and there. From Thanksgiving until Christmas, Walker helped out at Levi Swarey's Christmas tree farm in the mornings, cutting and baling trees and loading them onto *Englischers'* vehicles. The nearer Christmas drew, the more frantic the customers became, and Walker especially regretted leaving Levi short staffed on a Friday, their second busiest day of the week.

I imagine Roman bequeathed the haus *to Jane,* he thought as he guided his horse toward Main Street. He figured he ought to feel grateful, but instead the prospect overwhelmed him. Walker wasn't adept at negotiating legal matters and completing paperwork. Besides, the Lord had already provided him with a good living, and the house he shared with his daughter and mother had room to spare. *Either I'll have to sell the* haus *and put the money in a trust fund or rent it out until Jane becomes an adult and can decide for herself what to do with it.*

Walker didn't like picturing his daughter as an adult; she was growing too fast already. He smiled as he thought of her practicing for the annual Christmas program at school; she was so excited it was all she could talk about. Jane had been assigned three Bible verses to recite and although she'd memorized them thoroughly, she kept practicing, worried she might stutter or forget a word. *She probably developed that anxiety from being around her* groossdaadi. *Gloria's daed was so particular; everything had to be just right and even then, he was rarely satisfied.*

Walker immediately felt guilty for thinking ill of Roman. There was no doubt in his mind the man had loved Jane dearly and wanted the best for her. The problem was, Roman's sense of what was *best* often bordered on perfectionism. His standards were almost impossibly high and he had virtually no tolerance for mistakes, big or small. *If only he'd exhibited more mercy...* Walker shook the thought from his head, remembering one of his mother's oft-quoted sayings, "*If only* is a complaint dressed up as a wish."

As he journeyed through town, Walker spied a tree toppled in an *Englischer*'s front yard. It wasn't a large tree, but its weight was enough to splinter the nearby fence when it landed on it. *At least it's only wood that was fractured. A fence can be replaced.*

Just like that, the memory of the tree-trimming accident came rushing back, as instantaneously as the accident itself. One moment Walker had been strolling across a customer's lawn toward his employer's bucket truck. The next moment it felt as if he'd been knocked between the shoulder blades with an anvil. Then there was a black, blank void.

When he came to, Walker was in the hospital. His foreman explained one of the ropes the crew used to bring limbs down had snapped, causing a twelve-foot branch to swing in the wrong direction. Walker assumed the limb had knocked him flat, but he was told the force he'd felt against his back was his *Englisch* friend and co-worker, Jordan, shoving him out of harm's way. Although his helmet was cracked, Walker survived the accident with nothing more than a minor concussion. Jordan, unfortunately, suffered a broken neck and skull fracture and perished at the scene.

It had been eight years, but Walker still shuddered at the memory. Or maybe that was partly from the weather; it was definitely cold enough to snow. He pushed his hat down over his ears and worked the horse into a quicker trot.

Once he reached Main Street, he stopped to get out and hitch the horse to a post behind the library and then he jogged across the street to the attorney's office. The receptionist was on the phone, so he hung up his coat and hat and waited until she was free to usher him to the attorney's office.

"I'm Anthony Marino," the attorney said, extending his hand. "Have a seat. The other party should be here soon. Would you like something to drink? Coffee? Water?"

"No, thank you," Walker replied in *Eng-*

lisch. He sat down before repeating, "The other party?"

"Your father-in-law named two heirs for the majority of his estate," Anthony explained just as the receptionist tapped on the door. He crossed the room to open it, saying, "Looks like she's here now."

Because the woman was wearing a bonnet, Walker couldn't immediately see her face from where he was sitting. But after Anthony introduced himself, she replied, "And I'm Fern Glick. It's nice to meet you."

Walker gasped audibly and both Fern and Anthony swiveled their heads in his direction. Anthony chuckled, saying, "Obviously, there's no need for me to introduce the two of you."

Fern's eyes, which were as gray as the snow clouds outside the window, opened wide with apparent disorientation as she looked at Walker. He hardly had a chance to register that she still had a faint smattering of freckles across her nose and cheeks before she glanced away. *"Neh,"* she answered the attorney. "We're already acquainted."

Acquainted? The word was like a snowball right between Walker's eyes. *Acquainted?* They'd once pledged their undying love for each other! Of course, that was over eight years ago and they'd both married other people since then, but did Fern have to reduce their past relationship to nothing more than acquaintances? Walker tugged at his shirt collar, as if that would help him breathe better.

"Please, make yourself comfortable, Fern," the attorney said, gesturing to the chair next to Walker's.

As Anthony turned and emptied a decanter of ice water into two glasses, Fern perched on the far edge of her seat, her elbows pressed to her sides and her hands folded on her lap. She'd always had a way of drawing into herself, as if to take up as little space as possible, but today her posture seemed like a rebuff of Walker's presence. He tried to think of a greeting that wouldn't sound trite, but his tongue felt thick and his mind was woolly. He hadn't felt this unnerved since the first time he'd ever sat so close to Fern.

Anthony handed them each a glass and Walker gratefully took a gulp of water. The attorney sat down behind his desk and explained Roman had required both Walker and Fern to be present for the reading of his will. "I can go through the document with you word-by-word, but the long and short of it is that Roman named you two as beneficiaries of his estate."

"You mean he named Fern and my *dochder*, Jane, as beneficiaries, right?" Walker clarified.

"No, he actually bequeathed his possessions and estate to Fern and you, not to your daughter. Roman indicated he trusted you implicitly to do right by Jane."

That's surprising—he never said a complimentary word about my relationship with my dochder *when he was alive.*

Anthony added, "He also understood it would simplify things if he named you as a beneficiary because there are very precise stipulations to the inheritance."

Now that *sounds more like Roman.* "What are those stipulations?"

"First, Roman bequeathed the house solely to Fern for as long as she chooses to reside in it."

The brim of Fern's bonnet obscured her profile but Walker heard her inhale sharply. She leaned forward and placed her water glass on a coaster on Anthony's desk. "What if I don't choose to reside in it?"

"Then you may sell it. But in that case you and Walker will split the profit, fifty-fifty."

Fern's response was immediate and decisive. "That's what I'd like to do, then. Can you help me arrange the sale?"

Anthony balked. "I'd be glad to, but wouldn't you like to give it more thought? The last time I spoke with Roman, he led me to believe you didn't have your own—"

"I don't need to think it over," Fern interrupted. "I have absolutely no intention of living in Maine ever again."

What she means is she has no intention of living around me *ever again,* Walker thought.

"I care less about getting market value than I do about selling the house as soon as possible," Fern asserted. "I understand there are real estate investing franchises that can expedite a cash sale. I'd like to contact one of them."

Anthony picked up a pen and rolled it between his fingers. "That's fine, as long as Walker agrees. According to the conditions of the will, he has the first option of buying you out—"

"I'm not interested in acquiring another house," Walker objected. Eventually he'd just resell it, so it wasn't worth the added hassle of buying out Fern's share first.

"Okay, in that case the house becomes

joint property for you to sell. You'll have to agree on how you want to go about that."

Walker cleared his throat. "I'm not sure we should rush into working with an investing franchise instead of a local realtor. For one thing, it's a very big decision to make on the spot. For anoth—"

"You've made big decisions on the spot before," Fern broke in, staring directly at him. Her face, always thin, had become more angular with age. Or maybe it was her cutting remark—an obvious reference to his decision to marry Gloria— that made Fern's features appear sharper.

Clenching the water glass, he averted his eyes and addressed Anthony instead. "The other reason I think we should wait is that the recent ice storm brought down two trees in Roman's yard. One blocks the lane and the other clipped the edge of the *haus* and damaged the roof. We'll get a much better price for the property if we at least make that repair and clear the yard before we show it to prospective buyers, whoever they are. I could fix everything up myself within a couple of weeks."

The attorney leaned forward and spoke to Fern. "Walker's right. Even a real estate investing franchise is going to appraise the house before making an offer. A little yard work and a minor repair might make the difference between thousands of dollars." When Fern was silent, Anthony pressed, "May I ask why you're in such a hurry to sell?"

"I—I—I'm only going to be in Serenity Ridge until the twenty-third," Fern stammered. "I want to get the process started in person now and I can't always get to the phone shanty."

"That's no problem. I can mail you the necessary documents for signing when the time comes, and I'll give you my personal cell phone number so if you have questions, you can call me whenever it's convenient for you." Anthony smiled convincingly.

"Denki," Fern said. Walker noticed they both kept slipping in and out of *Deitsch*.

"Just a couple more things concerning Roman's estate," Anthony said, shuffling through his papers. "It looks like he left his livestock and buggy to the Fry family."

Sarah Fry had been widowed two years ago and she was struggling to feed her seven children, all under the age of twelve. After Roman's death in early November, the deacon tasked the two eldest Fry boys with caring for Roman's horse, milk cow and chickens at their home until the will was read. Walker was touched to learn Roman wanted them to have the animals and buggy permanently, as he knew how much it would benefit them. *I guess there was a side to him I didn't always see*, he admitted to himself.

"As for Roman's possessions in the house, stable and workshop, similar rules apply—Fern would have inherited them in full if she'd taken up residence. Since she's chosen not to, the two of you need to decide together what you'll do with the furnishings and tools, et cetera."

"I don't want anything from the *haus*, but if Walker does, he can take whatever he'd like. Otherwise, I think we should give the material goods to someone in need or include them in the sale of the house," Fern said.

Anthony rubbed his temples, clearly bewildered by her snap decision to forfeit any material goods. "You're already in town, so I'd urge you to take a look through the house and workshop first."

After a brief silence, Fern unexpectedly agreed. Walker was further taken aback when she questioned, "Since the *haus* is unoccupied, may my *kinner* and I stay in it for the week? The woman I'm visiting, Jaala, received unexpected company, so the extra room would be *wilkom*."

"That's fine, as long as Walker has no objections."

"No, no objections." Although the roof was damaged superficially, from what

Walker could see in passing, the house was structurally sound. "However, I'm starting a full-time contractor position after the first of the year, so if I'm going to work on Roman's *haus* and yard, I'll have to get started on it next week."

Wrinkling his forehead, Anthony shrugged. "I can't see that presenting a problem, will it, Fern?"

Fern's discernible pause indicated she thought otherwise, but she answered, "*Neh*. I'm sure we won't disturb one another."

Too late for that, Walker thought ruefully.

After Anthony handed her the house key and a folder of paperwork, Fern said goodbye and hurried into the restroom. She ran warm water over her hands, trying to gather her composure.

The attorney never mentioned anyone else would be attending the meeting, so Fern assumed Walker had already been informed of the terms of the will during a separate appointment. And while she expected she might have seen him from afar at church on Sunday, she'd planned to avoid coming within speaking distance of him. Or at least, she'd planned to stay far enough away so that she wouldn't have been able to smell the lemongrass soap he still used or to hear the rustle of his pant legs when he shifted in his chair the way she could in Anthony's office.

So any elation or gratitude she felt over what the inheritance would mean for her future was temporarily eclipsed by how unsettling it was to have to sit in such close proximity to Walker for the past fifteen minutes.

You're being lecherich, she told the mirror. It didn't matter; a tear trickled down her cheek anyway. Fern thought she'd forgiven Walker and moved on but the hurt, anger and confusion felt as raw and real today as they had felt eight years ago. Of all things, it had been his mustache that set it off again…

The Amish communities in Maine were among a handful in the country that permitted the men to wear mustaches, as well as beards, when they married. When Fern glimpsed Walker's dark, coppery-brown facial hair, which appeared as thick and soft-looking as the hair on his head, she remembered the secret signal he used to give her. When he was across the room at church or a singing, he'd stroke the skin beneath his nose with his index finger and thumb, as if smoothing an imaginary mustache. The gesture was his way of saying, "I can't wait to be married."

Oh, he couldn't wait to be married all right—just not to me! she fumed. Fern pulled a paper towel from the dispenser and dried her hands, then adjusted her bonnet. Stalling until she could be sure Walker had left the building, she idly thumbed through the folder of paperwork. She didn't even like seeing Walker's name and hers together on the same page. How was she going to endure being on the same property with him for the next seven days?

"Please, *Gott*, give me strength and grace," she whispered before exiting the restroom.

Fern could barely glance my way, much less greet me or say my name, Walker silently brooded as he drove toward the Christmas tree farm to begin his shift. *I understand why she'd resent me for marrying her* gschwischderkind, *but she doesn't know the full story.*

That was just it: *no one* knew the full story, except Walker. And he and Gloria had solemnly promised, for Jane's sake, they'd never tell another soul about what led to their sudden marriage shortly after the tree accident claimed his coworker's life.

As aggrieved as Walker had been by Jordan's death, he soon discovered Gloria was even more despondent. Walker knew Gloria and Jordan had socialized together—nearly eighteen, Gloria was still on her *rumspringa* and frequently hung out with *Englischers*—but he wasn't aware of the extent of their relationship until after the funeral. Walker was giving Gloria a ride home in his buggy when she broke down, confiding she was pregnant with Jordan's baby.

"We planned to get married next week on my birthday," she'd sobbed. "Now what will I do? My *daed* will never forgive me. He'll turn me out of the *haus* if I tell him about the *bobbel*."

Racked with guilt, Walker felt he couldn't allow Jordan's child to grow up homeless, as well as fatherless—not after the *Englischer* had given up his life to save Walker's. So, after intense agonizing, he sacrificed his own future for the baby's and wed Gloria instead of Fern. Although he believed he'd made an honorable decision, Walker was heartsick about ending his courtship with Fern, anticipating it would hurt her as much as it hurt him.

However, it appeared Fern's pain was short-lived; she hadn't even waited until the following autumn wedding season to marry Marshall. According to Jaala, they'd wed in the spring, a mere seven months after Fern told Walker she'd rather remain single forever than to pledge her life to any man other than him.

Granted, Walker had said the same thing to her. The difference was, despite all outward appearances, *he* had meant it. *I didn't* want *to marry Gloria, but at the time I didn't seem to have any other choice*, he rationalized. *If the shoe were on the other foot and Fern had been forced to marry someone else,* I *would have stayed single for the rest of* my *life...*

Which was exactly what he planned to do from now on, but it was no longer because he clung to any enduring love for Fern. On the contrary, his breakup with

Fern had taught him what a mistake it was to give his heart to her. To *any* woman.

Likewise, although Walker cherished Jane as much as any father cherished his daughter, in retrospect he realized he shouldn't have married Gloria. If he hadn't been so traumatized by the accident, Walker likely would have come up another way to help her and the baby that didn't involve keeping such a burdensome secret. That didn't involve living a lie.

I can't change the past, but with Gott's *help, I can make better decisions in the present*, he reminded himself as he turned down the lane to the Christmas tree farm. *And for the next week that includes keeping as much distance between Fern and me as she seems to want.*

Chapter Two

Filtered through a cloudy sky, the sunlight cast a white glare, and Fern squinted as she peered down Main Street toward the small *Englisch* market located on the other side of the bank. Shopping there was more expensive than at the superstore on the opposite side of town, but since she didn't want to walk that far in the cold from Roman's house with the children, Fern decided she'd better pick up some groceries now.

A jangling bell announced her arrival as she opened the door, but a quick scan of the aisles fortunately revealed the only

other people in the shop were *Englischers.*
Given her weepiness, it was better if Fern
didn't have to face someone else from her
past today. She selected beans, rice and
a few other staples from the shelves, but
she decided against buying flour or vegetables until she saw what Roman had left
over in his pantry and cellar. Since he'd
given away his livestock, Fern reluctantly
added a half gallon of milk and a dozen
eggs to her basket, too. Store-bought eggs
were never quite as tasty as those she
collected from the henhouse herself and
these were labeled Organic, which meant
they'd be twice as pricey as the kind sold
at the superstore. *I'll just have to cut back
somewhere else in our food budget*, she
decided.

By the time she got to Jaala's house,
it was flurrying. The children had their
mouths open to the sky as they attempted
to catch snowflakes on their tongues.

"Don't eat too many or you'll spoil your
appetites for lunch," Fern called, teasing.

Phillip and Patience immediately dashed over to give her a hug. She never tired of their fervent greetings, which more than made up for all the times she'd ever second-guessed how her relatives felt about having her live with them when she was a youth.

Jaala said her daughters-in-law were in the basement feeding the laundry through the wringing machine and her sons were in the workshop, so Fern took advantage of the opportunity to speak with Jaala in private, telling her about the meeting with the attorney and her plan to stay in Roman's house for the rest of her time in Serenity Ridge.

Jaala frowned. "Are you sure, dear? You don't have to leave on our account. The *kinner* are getting along so well. They're going to be terribly disappointed to be separated."

"They're *wilkom* to visit anytime. Roman has that big hill in the backyard—if the snow keeps up, the *kinner* can go sledding." Fern had no idea how she'd feed everyone if they came during lunchtime, but she'd think of something. For now, it felt good to be the one in the position of offering hospitality to someone else, even if staying in Roman's house was undoubtedly going to dredge up unpleasant memories.

After lunch, Fern fetched the suitcase she shared with Phillip and Patience. Jaala was right; all of the children were disappointed they were leaving, but they brightened when Fern invited Jaala's grandchildren to visit as soon as the snow was deep enough for sledding.

Since Abram had come home for his lunch break, he gave Fern, Phillip and Patience a ride to Roman's house on his way back to the lumberyard. Fern's stomach fluttered in nervous anticipation as they wound along the familiar roads toward her uncle's property on the outskirts of town. For most of her life, she had lived with relatives in large Amish settlements in Ohio or Pennsylvania, where she could look in any direction and see vast stretches of farmland punctuated by barns and silos. Not so in Serenity Ridge, where large stands of tall pine trees separated one family's property from another's. The hills in this part of Maine were steep and rocky, and because Serenity Ridge's Amish settlement was only about twenty-five years old, it was still a relatively small community—although Fern did notice several new Amish houses that hadn't been built when she lived there.

"You can see the ice storm did quite a bit of damage," Abram pointed out. "Tomorrow there's a frolic to repair the Blanks' *haus*, weather permitting. A tree crashed straight through two of their upstairs bedrooms and came to rest in the gathering room. Thank the Lord, no one was hurt."

"I'm told there are a couple of trees down in my *onkel* Roman's yard, too, but they didn't damage his *haus* much," Fern said.

Abram responded that there was a second work frolic the following weekend to repair the Schwartzes' barn, but he said he could arrange for the men to clean up Roman's yard on Saturday, December 30.

"*Denki*, but Walker is going to make the repairs in the afternoons during the upcoming week. He said it shouldn't take him long so the trees must have been fairly small."

But when they rounded the bend and Roman's yard came into view, Fern was surprised to see the size of the downed trees. One of them, a cedar, had completely uprooted and was blocking the driveway. The other, which was actually a large section of an oak tree, not the tree in its entirety, had split in such a way that the base of the branch was still partially attached to the trunk, although the rest of it had toppled over and was wedged against the ground, forming an upsidedown V with the tree. Smaller limbs littered the yard. *Roman would have hated how messy his lawn looks*, Fern thought.

Abram brought the suitcase to the porch before hurrying off to work. Fern was glad he didn't want to come inside; her stomach was still upset and she needed time to adjust to being back in her uncle's house again. Instead of taking the key out of her purse, she set her bag of groceries down, turned and motioned to the lawn. "You may play anywhere in the yard except under the tree by the side of the *haus*, okay?"

"*Jah*," the children agreed in unison.

"There's a big hill in the backyard and you're allowed to climb to the very top of it and run or sled all the way to the bottom, but you mustn't go into the woods without me," she instructed them. "Would you like me to show you around? We can look in the barn and in the workshop, too."

"I'm cold. Can we go inside?" The tip of Patience's nose was pink.

"*Jah*, I want to see what the *haus* looks like first," Phillip said, and Fern knew she couldn't put off entering it any longer.

"Sure, but we have to take our boots off at the door. There's no mudroom." She found herself automatically repeating the rule her uncle had frequently cited when she lived there, despite the fact she and Gloria were long past the age of needing a reminder not to dirty the floors. The children were so eager to get inside they pulled off their boots before she could steady her hands enough to turn the key in the lock.

The tiny square-shaped house opened to a small living room on the left and a staircase on the right. Still able to find her way through the house in the dark, Fern edged along the wall and pulled the shades up to let in more light. A small maroon sofa and matching armchair, as well as a rocker, were angled toward the woodstove. There was a round braided rug in the center of the floor and a smaller, rectangular braided rug near the door. Nothing hung on the walls except a single shelf just large enough to hold a clock. The clock's battery must have died because its hands read nine thirty-five. There was a gas-powered lamp built into a rolling table at one end of the sofa, and a Bible rested atop the flat surface. The wood bin was located at the opposite end, closest to the stove; it was still full.

There was a tradition among Serenity Ridge's Amish women to clean the house for the family of someone who had just died. Largely, this charitable act was done because after the funeral, the family was expected to host a gathering at their home. In Roman's case, Jaala and Abram had hosted a gathering at the church instead because the Serenity Ridge district, like the Amish community in nearby Unity, was unique in that its members met in a building for worship instead of in each other's homes. But Fern could tell by the faint scent of vinegar in the air the women had cleaned Roman's house anyway. Not that there would have been much to do—

he insisted on keeping everything extraordinarily tidy, even by Amish standards.

Phillip sat down on the sofa and bounced twice, testing the springs, whereas Patience stood in the middle of the room and turned a slow circle, tentatively taking in her surroundings.

"Kumme," Fern said to them after she got a fire going. "I'll show you the kitchen."

They followed her through the living room to the equally tiny kitchen. It housed a gas stove, a gas-powered refrigerator and a table with four chairs. Two additional chairs were in the corners of the room. Fern resisted the urge to peek in the cupboards to see what staples Roman still had on hand; she'd do that later, when the children weren't around. Patience was so perceptive she'd recognize her mother was taking inventory, and then the young girl would worry there wasn't enough for them to eat.

Next Fern showed the children where

the bathroom was, and then the three of them stuck their heads into Roman's bedroom across the hall. Fern's eyes stung as she recalled that immediately after Roman's stroke, she and Gloria had to wrap his arms around their necks to lift him from bed until he was capable of walking by himself again. *Those were such difficult days for him, yet they were some of the happiest for me because of how much I enjoyed living with Gloria. And because I'd just met Walker...*

"Let's go upstairs," she said quickly, brushing a tear from her cheek. The children hadn't uttered a word and she was concerned they were still upset about having to leave Jaala's to come to such a cold, empty shoebox of a house. *Maybe this was a mistake...*

There were two rooms at the top of the stairs; Fern pointed to the one on the right. "This used to be my room when I lived here," she told them, and Phillip pushed the door open farther and bounded inside.

"My *gschwischderkind*, Gloria, slept in the other one."

Patience hung back, her eyes as big as saucers. "You had a room just for yourself?"

"*Jah.*"

"Look at this, Patience. *Mamm* had her own double bed and a dresser and a chair! Her own closet, too," Phillip announced from inside the bedroom.

The children's astonishment troubled Fern. While she valued that they had learned at a young age how to share joyfully with others and to be satisfied with whatever God had given them, she wished they'd known what it was like to have a *little* more personal space—or at least a bed for themselves. *But that will change as soon as this* haus *sells and we can move out of Adam and Linda's home,* she thought. It was really starting to sink in that for the first time in her life she wouldn't have to be dependent on anyone else—and especially not on a man—for a place to live.

"Weren't you lonely sleeping by yourself?" Patience asked.

"Sometimes," Fern admitted. She understood her daughter's fear about sleeping alone, but she didn't want it to keep her from getting a good night's rest while they were there that week—or once she permanently had a bed to herself. "But I'd read or pray or else Gloria would tiptoe into my room and we'd talk until we were tired enough to fall asleep. And once you're sleeping, you're not lonely, are you?"

As she spoke, Fern had to fight back tears again, recalling her late-night chats with her cousin, which were sometimes serious, sometimes silly, and almost always involved secrets they didn't want Roman to hear. Three years younger than Fern, Gloria had also been an only child and she'd lost her mother as a girl, so in those ways the two young women had a lot in common. Even though they'd never met until Fern came to Maine, they bonded with each other immediately and grew even closer over time.

She was like my little schweschder, Fern recalled. But there wasn't an ounce of sibling rivalry between them. That was partly why it was so baffling and hurtful when Gloria married Walker. Fern hadn't ever told her cousin she was in love with Walker and planned to wed him that autumn—she and Walker had kept that a closely guarded secret. But Gloria was aware Walker had been Fern's suitor for over two and a half years, so she knew better than to enter into a courtship with him the moment Fern left for Ohio.

At least, that's when Fern initially *assumed* Walker and Gloria's relationship began. But after a while as she reflected on her cousin's behavior, she realized Gloria hadn't quite seemed herself that summer; she'd grown jumpy and secretive, as if she was hiding something.

As Fern stood in the hallway, she remembered the last late-night conversation she'd shared with her cousin. Much to Roman's consternation, Gloria was still on *rumspringa* and her father had told her either she had to put her running around period behind her and join the Amish church in the spring following her eighteenth birthday or she'd have to find somewhere else to live. That evening, Gloria was uncharacteristically doleful as she confided how conflicted she'd felt about making that decision.

"I don't know if I can be *gut* all the time the way we're required to be once we become members of the *kurrich*," she'd said.

"No one but *Gott* is *gut* all the time. The rest of us need the Holy Spirit to empower us not to sin and Christ's grace and forgiveness when we fail," Fern had replied. "If sin disqualified someone from joining the *kurrich*, there's not a person on earth who could join."

"*Jah*, but you don't know some of the

baremlich things I've done. The things I'm *tempted* to do…"

"Scripture says nothing can separate us from the love of God in Christ and that if we confess our sins, God is faithful to forgive us. It also says He'll provide a way of escape from temptation."

"That's just it. I don't know if I want to escape the things I'm tempted by…or if I'd rather escape the *Ordnung*," Gloria had mumbled before bursting into tears.

Back then, Fern had interpreted Gloria's hesitance to join the church as a reflection of how much pressure she felt to live up to her father's standards, not the Lord's. But in hindsight, Fern suspected getting involved with Walker romantically was one of the "terrible things" Gloria had alluded to doing or being tempted to do long before Fern went back to Geauga County that fall.

But Fern had never once noticed a change in Walker's behavior toward her. If anything, they'd become closer than ever that summer. Maybe he was better at covering it up than Gloria was, but if he had developed romantic feelings for her cousin that summer, why would he have suggested they get married in the fall? So Fern had concluded years ago that Walker and Gloria's relationship *had* to have started after she left for Ohio. *Out of sight, out of mind*, she thought sourly.

"Let's look in the other room," Phillip urged, tugging Patience's hand and pulling her back into the hall—and Fern's thoughts back into the present. He gallantly offered, "You can choose which one you want to sleep in."

But Patience didn't need to look at the other room to know she wanted to sleep in Fern's old room. "I can pretend I'm *Mamm* when she was a little *maedel*."

"I wasn't a little *maedel*, Patience. I lived here from the time I was eighteen until I was twenty-one."

"Then I can pretend I'm you when you

lived here and you were all growed up. I want to be just like you, *Mamm*."

Oh, sweetheart, I want more for your life than that. "Let's go get our things from the porch," she suggested. But before Phillip and Patience scampered down the stairs, her son threw his arms around Fern's waist.

"This is a great *haus*, *Mamm*!" he said. "It's got so much space and there aren't a lot of things we have to be careful not to bump into or break!"

"*Denki* for bringing us here," Patience added. "I wish we could stay till *Grischtdaag*."

With those few words, Fern's children utterly changed her perspective, as they'd frequently done throughout their young lives, just by being themselves. Fern may not have found the kind of love she'd once hoped for in a man, but she'd been blessed with two children she couldn't have imagined in her fondest dreams. A few tears rolled down her cheeks and when Patience noticed, she asked what was wrong.

"Nothing. I'm crying because I'm so grateful *Gott* gave you to me," she replied. *You're all the* familye *I'll ever need or want.*

Walker spied Jane standing on the steps of the one-room schoolhouse, licking her mitten. It had stopped flurrying but a dusting of snow—the first of the season—had collected on the railing and she must have wiped her hand over it so she could have a taste. Her lips and chin always got so chapped in winter from eating snow off her hands like an ice cream cone, but Walker had given up trying to dissuade her; she'd outgrow her childish antics too soon anyway. When she spotted him she clapped, ran across the yard and boarded the buggy.

"Guess how many days until our *Grischtdaag* program?" she asked as he tucked a blanket around her legs to keep her warm; the temperature seemed to have dropped a good seven degrees since that morning.

The annual school Christmas program was one of the Amish community's favorite traditions. The presentation included a Biblical recitation of the nativity story by the children, carols, a gift exchange and a wide array of seasonal refreshments. Usually it was held on the last weekday before December 25, but the teacher, Amity Speicher, had requested to go out of town for Christmas, so the school board decided to hold the program on Wednesday, December 20. Unlike *Englisch* children, Amish children usually didn't get a long Christmas break, but this year they'd have December 21 and 22 off, in addition to Monday, December 25.

Walker scratched his head, pretending not to know when the event would occur. "One hundred and eighteen?"

"*Daed!* How could there be one hundred and eighteen days left when there were only six days yesterday?" she asked incredulously.

"Aha! If there were only six days left yesterday, that means there are only five days left today," he deducted.

"You tricked me!" Jane accused him, but she laughed and he laughed, too. His dark-haired, pudgy-cheeked daughter's smile had that effect on him; even more so now because she was missing two teeth. Usually Walker thought she was the spitting image of Gloria, but every once in a while when she was overly tired and her eyelids were half-mast, she reminded him of Jordan. Although the similarity brought Walker comfort because it was like catching a glimpse of his *Englisch* friend's face, he was relieved no one in their community had known Jordan well enough to notice the resemblance.

"Want to hear me say my Bible verses?" Jane asked.

She had rehearsed saying them so many times, Walker knew them by heart himself, but he answered yes, so she recited Luke 2:9–11, which went:

And, lo, the angel of the Lord came upon them, and the glory of the Lord shone round about them: and they were sore afraid. And the angel said unto them, Fear not: for, behold, I bring you good tidings of great joy, which shall be to all people. For unto you is born this day in the city of David a Saviour, which is Christ the Lord.

When she finished, she asked, "Now do you want to practice 'Hark! The Herald Angels Sing' with me, *Daed*?"

The pair sang the rest of the way to their home, which was located on the west side of town close to an *Englisch* neighborhood. Walker had built the house the spring after he married Gloria; until then, he'd been living with his mother, Louisa, and sister, Willa, in his childhood home. Walker's father had died when Walker was sixteen, and his two older brothers had long since married. One moved to Fort Fairfield, a small settlement in the northern part of the state, and the other relocated to Canada.

After Gloria and Walker's wedding, the couple rented a *daadi haus* until Walker could build his current home. Then his sister got married the following year and she moved to the district in Unity, a neighboring town, so his mother sold the family house and went to live with Willa and her husband. When Gloria died, Louisa moved back to Serenity Ridge so she could help Walker raise Jane. She was the closest person to a mother Jane could remember, and Walker didn't know what he would have done without her help. Although he sometimes felt guilty about allowing her to believe he was Jane's biological father, Walker knew telling Louisa the truth wouldn't change one thing about his mother's relationship with Jane or decrease her love for the child.

Mamm has been more of a groossmammi *to Jane than Jordan's* mamm *ever was,* he thought. Gloria had visited Jordan's parents shortly after the funeral to tell them about her pregnancy, but they'd accused her of lying and said they wanted nothing to do with her or the baby. Their rejection of their son's child was another reason Walker felt compelled to marry Gloria.

As he and his daughter lifted their voices in song, he couldn't help but think, *Poor Jane. She might not have any of my genes, but she's as tone-deaf as I am!* It delighted him that they both belted out the carols anyway.

"*Groossmammi,* do you want to hear me recite my verses?" Jane asked the moment she got in the door. Another round of caroling followed and then a third round after supper.

Once Jane went to bed, Louisa invited Walker to have a cup of chamomile tea in the gathering room. Since the tree farm had been so busy that day and Walker had missed half his morning shift, he'd stayed there until it was time to pick Jane up, so he hadn't had a chance to tell his mother about the meeting.

"What did the attorney have to say?" she questioned. "Did Roman bequeath the *haus* to Jane?"

"*Neh*. He actually bequeathed it to me on her behalf."

"Ah, that makes sense."

"But he named a co-heir. His niece, Fern Troyer—I mean, Fern Glick." Walker lowered his eyes to blow on his tea so he wouldn't have to look at his mother. Because the Amish were customarily discreet about who they were courting, he'd never told his mother he was Fern's suitor. But he'd frequently sensed his mother suspected they were courting, and he didn't want his expression to give it away now.

His mother nodded. "That's as it should be. Fern is his relative, too, and she was such a blessing to him after he had the stroke. Gloria wouldn't have been able to manage his care on her own."

Walker remembered how often Gloria used to tell him the same thing. "Fern coming to live with us was the best thing that could have happened to me," she'd say. "Not only did she help enormously during *Daed*'s illness, but she was like a *schweschder* and a *mamm* and a best *freind* all rolled into one. I was so glad she stayed with us in Serenity Ridge even after *Daed* recovered."

I was so glad, too...

"Walker?" His mother interrupted his thoughts. "What's wrong?"

"Nothing." Walker hadn't realized he'd been glowering. His mother probably thought she'd made him lonely by mentioning Gloria, but really it was the memory of his and Gloria's broken relationships with Fern that saddened him. He had disciplined himself not to dwell on it over the years, but seeing her again had brought the regret to the forefront of his mind. "Anyway, neither Fern nor I want the *haus* for ourselves, so we're going to—"

"When did you speak to Fern?"

"This morning. She was there, at the attorney's office."

"Oh, that's *wunderbaar*! How are she and her *kinner* doing?"

Walker shrugged. "Fine, I guess. I don't really know."

"You didn't inquire about her *kinner* or her life in Ohio?"

She probably wouldn't have answered me if I did. "It wasn't the right time or place, *Mamm*. We were there to discuss the will. Afterward she darted off to the restroom and I had to hurry back to work."

"I'm surprised at you, *suh*. There's always enough time to catch up with a *freind*," his mother admonished him. "Especially when it's someone like Fern. She was such a tenderhearted *maedel* and the two of you got on well, if I recall. I even used to think you were courting her... I remember one time after *kurrich*, Roman told me he'd caught you sneaking down his lane in your buggy. I was sure you'd been there dropping off Fern, not Gloria."

Walker furrowed his brows. He and Fern had been even more discreet about their courtship than most Amish couples, mostly because they didn't know how Roman would react if he found out. There was nothing wrong with Walker being Fern's suitor, since they started courting when they were both eighteen and their behavior was completely respectable. But Fern always insisted Walker drop her off at the end of her street, even in the rain. It used to drive him crazy. "I won't melt," she'd coyly tease after they'd kissed good-night. "I'm already melted."

"I—I don't remember that," he said honestly, referring to Roman seeing him near the house. "I'm fortunate he didn't chase me off the property with a garden hoe."

"Oh, Roman wasn't that strict. He was just looking out for his *dochder*'s best interests," his mother said, causing Walker to swallow his tea wrong. He coughed into his sleeve as his mother asked, "Where is Fern staying while she's here?"

"She was at Jaala's *haus*, but now she and the *kinner* are going to spend the week at Roman's place."

"Didn't you tell me a tree hit his *haus*?"

"Grazed it, *jah*. It's only superficially damaged. A couple shingles missing from the roof, that's all. I'll patch it up this week and chop up the tree for firewood, too. Fern wants to put the *haus* on the market as soon as possible so I've got to get it ready for an appraisal and inspection."

"You ought to get started tomorrow, then. Jane will be thrilled to meet her *gschwischderkinner*. I'll bring a pie and we can all have lunch together."

Walker wiggled his leg. "*Neh*, we can't do that. There's a frolic at the Blanks' *haus*, remember?"

His mother's shoulders drooped. "Ach. I forgot. I don't know where my mind is. We'll have to visit her for supper on *Sunndaag* instead."

"I—I don't think that's a *gut* idea. You know how tiny Roman's *haus* is." When his mother squinted at him, Walker realized how unconvincing his excuse sounded. He embellished it, reasoning, "Besides, Fern is only here for a week. Roman left the *gaul* and buggy to the Fry *familye* so she doesn't have transportation to the grocery store. She probably won't have enough leftovers to feed us supper on the *Sabbat*. I don't want to embarrass her."

"Oh dear, you're right. Better we should invite her and the *kinner* here, instead."

"*Neh!*" Walker uttered.

His mother set her teacup in its saucer and cocked her head at him. "What in the world is wrong with you, *suh*? Fern was a member of our *kurrich* and she and her *kinner* are the only relatives Jane has left from Gloria's side of the *familye*. Why wouldn't you want them to meet each other?"

"I—I—I—" Walker's cheeks were blazing. For lack of any other plausible excuse, he said, "If I'm helping you host Fern and her *kinner*, I can't go for a walk with Eleanor Sutter on *Sunndaag*."

His mother pulled her chin back as if she couldn't believe her ears. Walker didn't blame her; he couldn't believe his *mouth*. But that's what happened when he was desperate—he panicked and made a rash decision.

Louisa replied, "You go ahead and have *schpass*. I'll host Fern and the *kinner* myself, but you'll have to give us all a ride home before you pick up Eleanor."

Why didn't I think of that before I opened my big mouth? My entire purpose in going for a walk with Eleanor after kurrich *was so I could avoid any close contact with Fern.* Walker wished he could take it back, but it was too late to change his plans now. "Okay."

As he rose to leave the room, his mother

beamed at him. "It's *wunderbaar* you're going to try courting again, *suh*."

"Going for a walk with a woman isn't the same thing as *walking out* with her, *Mamm*," he emphasized.

Despite his mother's pronounced hinting over the past several years, Walker had adamantly refused to even consider courting anyone again. What was the point, since he had no intention of remarrying? But if he ever *had* been open to the possibility of a courtship, it most definitely wouldn't have been with Eleanor Sutter, whom he found to be immature, gossipy and prone to complaining.

Oh well. Spending an afternoon with her wouldn't be nearly as uncomfortable as spending an afternoon with Fern. At least, he hoped it wouldn't.

Chapter Three

Fern woke on Saturday to the sound of her own stomach growling. The evening before she'd been disappointed to find Roman's pantry and cellar were completely bare. No canned fruit or vegetables, no salt or sugar, not even any flour for making bread. Uncertain if or when anyone would be visiting the house again, the women in the district had probably cleared the house of all foodstuff so it wouldn't spoil or so mice wouldn't get into it. *But that means there's less variety of food for me to feed* my *two little mice until we go to town on* Muundaag, Fern fretted as she gazed at Phillip and Patience asleep on either side of her.

Patience had gotten out of bed almost immediately after Fern tucked her in on Friday, claiming she'd heard something knocking against the rooftop and she was afraid another tree was about to fall. So Fern had given her permission to sleep downstairs for the night, planning to show her in the morning how sturdy the trees were. When Phillip learned he'd be the only one sleeping upstairs, he came into Fern's bed, too. Fern didn't want to make it a habit, but oddly, despite being elbowed in the ribs by Phillip and crowded by Patience, she had one of the best night's sleep she'd had in years.

She tried to ease out of bed but as soon as she sat up, Phillip popped upright, too. "*Guder mariye, Mamm.* Are we going to explore the yard today?"

She tousled his hair and replied in a hushed tone, "After breakfast and chores."

"What chores, *Mamm*?" Patience opened

her eyes slowly. "There aren't any *hinkel* and this *haus* is so clean we can eat on the floor."

Fern suppressed a giggle at Patience's phrasing of the idiom. "There are a lot of fallen branches we need to pick up in the yard."

"If we find pine branches, can we decorate the *haus* for *Grischtdaag*? They don't cost any money. Please, *Mamm*?"

Fern winced; Phillip was too young to be so conscientious about their financial circumstances. "We won't be staying here until *Grischtdaag*. We're going back to Ohio next Saturday, which is December 23. But I suppose we can decorate anyway, as long as we take everything down before we leave."

After eating plain scrambled eggs for breakfast, the trio tromped outside. Patience and Phillip retrieved branches and twigs that had come down in the ice storm and brought them to Fern, who snapped them into smaller pieces and then stacked them in a heap beside the woodpile. Once they cleared the front section on the right side of the house, Fern suggested they trek up the hill in the backyard.

As they walked, Fern told the children about how she and Gloria would hike to the edge of the woods after they'd finished their morning shifts as housekeepers at the *Englisch* inn down the road. There was a large domed boulder there and they'd climb atop it with a picnic lunch. Afterward they'd take a shortcut through the woods to buy double-scoop cones of chocolate fudge brownie and cotton candy ice cream from a little Amish ice cream stand off of the main highway.

"Can *we* hike through the woods to get ice cream after lunch?" Phillip asked.

"*Neh, lappich*, it's too cold—the ice cream stand is closed for the winter," Fern said lightly, but the thought of it made her mouth water, too, especially since they were going to be eating eggs, beans and rice all weekend.

Fern realized Jaala had probably thought it would have been unfair to suggest the three of them attend the work frolic since they were only visiting, but Fern wished they'd been included. She knew what a delectable assortment of food the women would put out for everyone who came to help. Maybe there would be leftovers and they'd bring them to *kurrich* tomorrow. But even if there weren't leftovers, Fern was looking forward to the traditional after-church lunch, which consisted of cold cuts, cheese, church peanut butter, bread, pickles and pickled beets, homemade pretzels and dessert.

"Jaala usually brings spice *kuche* with cream cheese frosting to *kurrich*," she said, partly to herself and partly to the children. "We'll enjoy an *appenditlich* dessert tomorrow."

"Okay," Phillip agreed so good-naturedly it made Fern wish she could buy him an entire gallon of ice cream. "I want to roll down the hill anyway!"

"Be careful," Fern warned. "The ground's frozen."

Phillip had already dropped to his side. Bending his arms tightly against his chest, he spiraled down the hill like a log. Patience remained upright, traipsing behind him while clasping Fern's hand. At the bottom, they waited until Phillip regained his balance before they scoured the perimeter of the yard for fallen pine boughs and cones to decorate the windowsills, as well as to make a wreath.

They also collected wire, glue and fishing line from Roman's workshop. The Amish generally didn't embellish their Christmas greenery with elaborate bows or tinsel, but Fern decided their wreath needed a touch of color. So after lunch, she took the children across the road and down a hill toward a swampy area to search for wild winterberries.

"Sometimes moose like to roam in this area," she informed them. "They don't like to be frightened, so we should sing

Grischtdaag carols, and that way they'll hear us coming."

They spotted the stunning red berries before they'd even finished singing the second stanza of "Joy to the World," and in no time they'd collected enough to brighten the wreath and tuck into the boughs they'd arrayed across the windowsills. To their delight, Fern found candles—admittedly, in mismatched heights and shapes—in one of Roman's kitchen drawers. After carefully securing them among the arrangements on the sills, she lit their wicks and then hung the wreath on the door.

As the trio stood on the porch and admired their handiwork, Patience breathlessly exclaimed, "It's too bad *Onkel* Adam and *Ant* Linda and Emma and Thomas and Benjamin and Miriam and the *bobbel* can't see how pretty our *haus* looks."

Fern fought the impulse to remind her daughter they were only staying there temporarily. Instead, she suggested, "Maybe you and Phillip could draw pictures of the *haus* to show to your *gschwischderkinner* when we get back to Ohio. But first we need to eat supper."

After their meal—this time Fern served fried eggs with their rice and beans—she did the dishes as the children drew on the back of the junk mail envelopes Fern had pulled from the box earlier that afternoon, since that was the only paper she could find. Then she gave each child a bath and put them to bed in their own rooms. All the outdoor activity must have worn them out because they fell asleep without any fuss.

After bathing and washing her own hair, Fern retreated to the living room to read from her uncle's Bible. It was so quiet that each time she turned a page, she was keenly aware of the sound of the paper rustling. For as often as she wished she and the children had a space of their own, Fern found herself longing for another adult to talk to, and by the end of the evening she could hardly wait to go to church—even if it did mean she might cross paths with Walker again.

Sunday dawned warmer than usual, which made walking to church especially pleasant. Fern, Phillip and Patience had just arrived and were hanging up their coats in the foyer when a voice from behind them asked, "Fern, is that you?"

She turned to find Walker's mother standing behind her with outstretched arms. "Hello, Louisa," she replied, giving her a swift embrace.

Fern had always liked Walker's mother, but she was concerned that if Louisa had just arrived, it meant Walker couldn't be far behind. Usually the men and women entered the church and sat separately during worship services in her district in Ohio, but here in Maine, the families sat together. Figuring Walker had dropped Louisa off near the door, Fern inched backward, hoping to take a seat before he entered the building, but Louisa had her cornered.

"I was so surprised to hear you were in town. I'm sorry it was a sad situation that brought you here, but I'm glad to see you again."

Fern couldn't honestly say she was glad to be there, so instead she replied, "*Denki*. It's *gut* to see you, too." Then she introduced Phillip and Patience to Louisa.

"Your *gschwischderkind*, Jane, can't wait to meet you," the older woman told them and gestured toward the door off to their left. "Here she comes with her *daed*."

Fern mechanically turned toward the door. When she saw the little girl holding Walker's hand, her breath snagged and her knees went soft. Despite the age difference, Fern felt as if she could have been looking at her cousin, instead of at her cousin's daughter; Jane's dark hair, round face and pert brown eyes were identical to Gloria's.

"Jane, this is Fern, your *mamm*'s *gschwischderkind* I was telling you about."

"*Guder mariye,*" Jane replied cheerfully, revealing two missing teeth when she grinned. Walker added his greeting to his daughter's, but Fern could scarcely reply to either of them. Seeing Jane had simultaneously sparked loneliness for her cousin and anger at both Gloria and Walker. As irrational as the notion was, especially in light of how she felt toward Walker now, Fern couldn't help thinking, *This was supposed to be* my kind *with Walker, not Gloria's.*

"*Guder mariye,*" Fern finally repeated. She pulled Patience and Phillip in front of her body, like a shield. "This is my *dochder*, Patience. And this is my *suh*, Phillip. *Kinner*, meet Jane, your *gschwischderkind.*"

The children said hello to each other and then Phillip gazed up at Walker. "Are you our *onkel*?"

"*Neh.* Walker is Jane's *daed* but he's no

relation to us." Fern spat out the words as if they burned her tongue. "Not like your *onkel* Adam is anyway. You should just call him Walker."

Walker could hear the indignation in Fern's voice when Phillip mistook him for being the children's uncle, but he tried to shrug it off. "Hello, Patience. Hi, Phillip," he said to the two small children, and their warm replies compensated for Fern's frostiness.

With her pale complexion, wispy stature and gentle smile, Patience was definitely Fern's daughter. But Phillip looked nothing like her. *He must take after his* daed, Walker assumed. Judging from the boy's dark, curly hair and healthy physique, Walker could only guess Fern's husband had been handsome and strong. Hadn't Jaala once mentioned he worked in construction? A stab of envy caught Walker off guard and his jaw went tight.

"I'm pleased we caught up with you before anyone else did," Walker's mother said. "We'd like you to *kumme* to our *haus* after *kurrich* so the *kinner* can get to know each other better."

Fern visibly blanched. "I—we—we—" she stammered.

Louisa seemed oblivious to her discomfort. "I'd love to hear about your life in Ohio. It will just be us women, though, since Walker is going—"

"Hiking," Walker cut in, mortified at the possibility his mother may have been on the brink of telling Fern he was going for a walk with Eleanor.

When Fern still didn't accept the invitation, Louisa added, "I made a peanut butter cream pie just for the occasion."

"Peanut butter cream pie?" Phillip marveled. "That's my favorite pie in the world."

Fern placed her hand on his head. "You mustn't interrupt adult conversation, *suh*," she said.

"I'm sorry, *Mamm*. My mouth made me

interrupt because it loves the taste of peanut butter cream pie so much."

Fern's cheeks pinkened but Walker's mother let out a hearty chuckle. "Then that settles it, doesn't it, Fern?" she pushed.

Walker was incredulous. *Can't* Mamm *see how reluctant Fern is to* kumme *to our* haus?

"*Denki*, we'd enjoy that," Fern politely conceded. "Excuse me, but I need to use the restroom before worship service begins. *Kumme*, Phillip and Patience."

Just like yesterday, Fern couldn't seem to get away from Walker quickly enough. *It's not as if I want to keep company with her, either*, he thought.

"I'll take your *kinner* inside with me so you can have your privacy," his mother offered. "We usually sit in the fourth or fifth row from the back on the right side of the aisle."

Walker recognized the look of alarm in Fern's eyes, but she deferred to his mother's authoritative tone. *"Denki,"* she said and bustled toward the stairwell.

"I'll show you the bench I like best because it's near the window." Without a moment's hesitation Jane took Patience's hand as if they'd been friends all their lives. Phillip followed the two girls and Louisa followed him, which put Walker at the end of the line.

He assumed that was the same order they'd sit on the bench, but instead his mother commented over her shoulder, "I'll sit on the far side so we can sandwich the *kinner* between us and keep an eye on them."

Once Fern sees me at this end, she'll go sit on the other side of Mamm, Walker assured himself. But right before Fern returned, an elderly couple, the Knepps, took a seat next to Louisa, so there was nowhere else Fern could sit except next to Walker. The group already occupied almost the entire bench as it was, so he shifted closer to Phillip in order to give

Fern more room. She folded into herself as usual, taking up no more space on the bench than her son, but she was still close enough for Walker to smell the lavender scent of her shampoo. He quickly redirected his focus to the worship service.

A few minutes after the singing ended and the sermon had begun, Phillip put his hands flat on either side of his legs and pushed his arms straight, lifting his feet from the floor and his bottom from the bench. He balanced this way for an impressive amount of time before his arms gave out and he dropped onto his backside again, jostling his sister beside him. The commotion caught Fern's attention and she leaned forward to peer down the aisle, waving a finger at her son. Phillip sat straight up again and so did Fern.

Walker gave her a sidelong look. Now that she was only wearing a *kapp* instead of a bonnet, he could take in her profile, which, save for a line or two cupping her pale pink lips, hadn't changed since he'd last seen her. From her flaxen-blond hair to her equally light eyebrows and eyelashes to the sprinkle of freckles across her straight nose, almost everything about Fern's face was understated. Everything except for her big gray eyes. Depending on her mood, they sometimes appeared flinty and cold, but more often than not, Fern's eyes glimmered like polished silver. "Like precious coins," he used to describe them. Walker jiggled his knee; he usually hung on every word of the sermon but today he was impatient for it to end. Being so close to Fern was unnerving him.

"Your *mamm* is going to scold you if you keep fidgeting like that," Phillip whispered loud enough for everyone around them to hear. Fern immediately bent forward to see past Walker again, a finger pressed to her lips. In response, Phillip slapped his hands over his mouth, bunched his shoulders to his ears and nodded affirmatively.

Walker stopped shaking his leg but laughter gripped him from the belly upward and he had to bite the inside of his cheek to keep it from escaping his lips. The more he tried to control his amusement at Phillip's mischievousness—or maybe it was just nervous laughter—the harder his body quaked. Fern, meanwhile, was posed as rigidly as a statue. *She must think I'm setting a* baremlich *example.*

Walker could sense Phillip's eyes on him, so he looked down and winked. Phillip grinned. Then, when Walker set his mouth in a serious line, crossed his arms over his chest and lifted his face toward the deacon, the boy copied him. *No matter how I feel about his* eldre, *I really like this* bu, Walker thought.

After the service, the three children took off to play outside with Jaala's grandchildren, and Fern and Louisa went downstairs to the kitchen to help prepare lunch. Walker helped the other men stack the benches atop each other so they could be used as tables the *leit* would stand around as they ate. Then he headed outside to see if the two men in charge of watering and feeding the horses that week needed any help, but he happened to spot Eleanor on the top landing of the stairs. Not surprisingly, she was loitering with her eyes closed and her head tipped toward the sun instead of assisting the other women with the food preparation.

Walker regretted that he was going to have to ask to pick her up later instead of offering to give her a ride home from church and stopping on the way to take a hike. Somehow, calling on her at home made it seem more deliberate. More like a date.

"It's a pretty day," he remarked awkwardly. "Warm."

She opened her eyes and blinked at him. Or was she batting her lashes? "*Jah*, it is. I've had a cold so I'm soaking in some vitamin D."

"I thought it was vitamin C you were

supposed to take when you had a cold."
Walker hadn't asked a woman to spend
the afternoon with him since...since he'd
courted *Fern*, but it wasn't nerves that was
making him procrastinate like this. It was
dread.

Eleanor, who was nearly as tall as he
was, nudged his shoulder. "Sunshine
doesn't have vitamin C in it, *schnickel-
fritz*."

"I know. That's what I meant—" Walker
didn't bother to explain further. Taking
a deep breath, he forged ahead, saying,
"Since today might be the last of the nice
weather, would you like to go for a ride
to Serenity Lake? We could take a walk
on the trail through the woods."

Eleanor lifted her eyebrows. "*Jah*. Walking with Walker—what a way to while
away the day!" she said, giggling at herself.

Walker was already getting a headache.
"I'll pick you up at two. Would you mind

meeting me at the end of your lane, near Pinewood Street?"

Eleanor bobbed her chin up and down. "Ah, I get it, you don't want anyone to know we're courting."

Courting? I never said anything about courting. "Neh!" he protested. "I mean, *jah*, you're right, I don't want anyone to know that I'm picking you up, but—"

Eleanor's brother, Henry, hopped through the door at that moment. "Hey, Walker. Do you want to go hunting with Otto and me? It's the last weekend of expanded archery season and Otto said he'd show us how to use his compound bow."

Walker wasn't especially interested in learning to use the bow, since he couldn't imagine himself ever buying one, but tagging along in the woods with Henry and Otto would have been preferable to spending the afternoon with Eleanor. Or with Fern. Once again, he realized in his haste to avoid an unpleasant situation, he'd missed out on a better opportunity that would have accomplished the same purpose. *When will I learn?*

"He can't," Eleanor piped up. "He's going for a hike with me."

For crying out loud! Walker should have known there was no need to worry about other people seeing him alone with Eleanor and spreading gossip—she'd beat them to the punch.

"Voll schpass," Henry said, implying his sister was joking. He knuckled Eleanor's arm as if they were Jane's age instead of in their twenties. "So, how about it, Walker?"

"I—uh—I really am going on a hike with Eleanor," Walker admitted.

Henry's mouth dropped open. "Oh. Okay..."

"You're *wilkom* to join us."

"He is not!" Eleanor objected.

"I already told Otto I'd go with him," Henry said. Then lifted his nose in the air. "Smells like they're bringing the food upstairs. I'm going inside to grab a spot at the table."

"I'll *kumme*, too." Although the *leit* sat together with their families during church, the men and women ate lunch separately afterward, and Walker was glad for the excuse to get away from Eleanor.

"See you at two o'clock," she said with an exaggerated wink. "I can't wait."

"See you," Walker muttered.

After Fern helped serve lunch to the men and children, she took a place at a table with Jaala and Jaala's daughters-in-law. She'd briefly caught up with some of the other women she used to know as they were preparing the meal together, and she supposed she ought to get to know the newer members of the district, too, but she felt emotionally spent and she still had a long afternoon ahead of her. As the women around her chatted vivaciously, Fern wondered, *How did I get roped into going to Walker's haus?*

She knew the answer. It wasn't politeness that had kept her from turning down Louisa's invitation; it was peanut butter cream pie. Fern didn't want to deny her son the pleasure of eating something he loved so much, something he never got to indulge in at Adam's because Emma was allergic to peanut butter. Besides, Fern understood why the children wanted to play with their cousin, and she didn't mind spending the afternoon with Louisa, either. But what vexed her was *where* they'd be spending it.

Before Walker broke up with Fern, they'd take long walks through the woods or sit on the shoreline of Serenity Lake, daydreaming about the house he'd build for her once they were married. He'd even sketch its design in the sand with a stick. And then he'd draw a garden in the front yard that contained flowers nearly as tall as the house itself because Fern once told him that when she was young she rarely lived anywhere long enough to see the gardens she'd helped plant come up the following year.

It was upsetting enough to meet the dochder *Walker had with Gloria*, she lamented. *Now I have to spend time in the* haus *he built for Gloria? It's like rubbing my nose in the fact he married her, not me.*

Fern instantly felt terrible for having such thoughts. *What kind of petty person begrudges her deceased* gschwischder- kind *a* haus*? Besides, Walker didn't invite us over—Louisa did. And she never knew anything about my courtship with him, so it's not really that anyone is trying to make me feel bad.*

"Are those beets too vinegary?" Jaala asked, causing Fern to realize she had puckered her mouth into a knot.

"*Neh*, they're *gut*," she answered. But after eagerly anticipating lunch since the day before, Fern had suddenly lost her appetite and she struggled to finish her meal.

A few minutes later as she and Walker's mother herded the children across the lawn toward his buggy, Louisa directed, "You sit up front with Walker. I'll join the *kinner.*"

Fern would have preferred to run alongside the horse rather than to sit next to Walker again today, but out of respect for Louisa's age, she acquiesced. *If I made it through a three-hour* kurrich *service sitting next to him, I can survive a short ride to his* haus.

As they began rolling down the steep hill, Fern strained to hear what was happening in the back seat; Jane's voice was barely audible as she recited the verses she'd learned for her school's Christmas program to Louisa, Phillip and Patience.

"I wonder if Serenity Ridge will have a white *Grischtdaag* this year," she heard herself saying absently.

"We might. It flurried on *Freidaag* and I'm told there could be a nor'easter headed our way toward the end of the week, but I'd never guess it judging from how warm it is today," Walker replied, briefly twisting in her direction.

Fern had always thought he looked especially handsome in his dark winter wool hat, but now his neatly trimmed sideburns, mustache and beard gave his rectangular-shaped face a maturity he hadn't had before, and their burnished color made his green eyes appear more vivid than ever. She shivered, despite the warmth of the sunshine streaming in through the buggy's storm front.

Flustered, she babbled, "I'm glad it's so nice out—it means the *kinner* will be able to run around outside and burn off some of their energy. I'm sorry if Phillip distracted you in *kurrich* today. He has a hard time sitting still."

Walker chuckled. "That's to be expected for a *bu* his age, especially one who is so athletic. He's strong, too—he must take after his *daed*."

"*Jah*, he does. I—I mean he *did*... I mean *jah*, he's husky and tall like Marshall was." Fern didn't know why, but she felt uncomfortable talking about her former husband with Walker. She'd feel even more uncomfortable talking about *Gloria* with Walker, but she recognized she somehow ought to acknowledge her cousin's passing. It would have been odd to offer condolences, especially after so much time, so instead Fern touched on the subject indirectly by remarking, "Jane is very sweet. She looks exactly like Gloria did."

"I think so, too," Walker agreed. "And Patience looks exactly like you. She has your eyes."

It was undoubtedly intended to be an innocuous comment, but it made Fern recall how Walker used to compliment her on the color of her eyes. "They're so silvery they shimmer," he'd say. "It's as if they're lit from inside."

"If that's true, it's only because they reflect how *hallich* I feel whenever I'm with you," she'd banter back, unabashedly saccharine.

But that was ages ago. Fern was a different person now, and if her eyes reflected anything it was how overwhelmed she was. She had expected that coming back to Serenity Ridge and facing the past would be difficult, but she didn't think it would be *this* difficult. And she certainly didn't think she'd have to make small talk with Walker about their children or the weather, as if nothing had ever happened between them. As if Walker hadn't shattered her heart to bits.

Just then, Patience's melodic giggle rose from the back of the buggy, followed by Phillip's boisterous laughter, and then Jane said something Fern couldn't quite hear but it caused everyone to laugh harder.

It's only one afternoon, Fern reminded herself. *And I'm doing it for the* kinner. She could do just about anything for her children.

* * *

Walker noticed Fern recoiling from his remark. He sensed he shouldn't have expressed his observation about Patience's eyes being like her mother's, but he wasn't sure why not. It was meant to be a compliment, but clearly Fern didn't take it that way; she shifted in her seat to stare out the other side of the buggy and journeyed the rest of the way in silence.

Once they reached the house, Walker let everyone off in front before continuing down the long driveway toward the barn. There was no sense unhitching Daisy because Walker was only going to run into the house and change out of his church clothes before leaving again. When he was courting Fern and they'd go for a walk after church, Walker always stayed in his best Sunday attire, but today he didn't want anyone—least of all, *Eleanor*—to get the impression he was behaving the way a potential suitor would behave toward a woman he wanted to court.

He replenished the wood bin and stoked the fire before bidding goodbye to his mother and Fern, who were already sipping tea in the living room. Outside, he carefully navigated the buggy past Jane, who was letting Patience and Phillip take turns riding her yellow scooter up and down their paved driveway. While he loved how welcoming and generous his daughter was, Walker hoped she wouldn't get too attached to Fern's children; after today, he didn't want them playing together. Mostly because he didn't want to have to spend another afternoon with Fern. Nor did he want to have to spend another afternoon *avoiding* Fern.

Especially not if it meant hanging out with Eleanor, who seemed determined to extend her time with Walker for as long as possible. Once they got to the lake, she tiptoed along the path through the woods at a snail's pace, regaling him with a story about helping her nephew memorize his verses for the Christmas program. Even after they'd reached the water and scaled a large, flat boulder that provided the perfect vantage point for viewing Serenity Lake, she blathered on and on.

Walker alternately murmured "hmm" or chuckled when it seemed she was waiting for his response. But his mind was light-years away as he recalled stargazing from this very rock with Fern shortly before she left for Ohio. They'd had a rare argument because Walker didn't want her to go but Fern maintained her aunt had no one else to care for her. Which wasn't exactly true—she had her son, Adam, but at the time he was still on his *rumspringa* and was living out his rebellion among the *Englisch* somewhere in Dayton.

"You know what *Gott*'s word says about caring for people in need, especially in our *familye*," Fern had wept. "Please understand why I have to do this, Walker."

Walker *had* understood. Fern's sacrificial care for those who were sick and help for those who needed help was one of the qualities he'd loved most in her. "Just promise you won't stop loving me while you're gone."

"I'll *never* stop loving you," she'd claimed and Walker had believed her. But that was before his world literally came crashing down around him…

"Yoo-hoo," Eleanor sang, snapping her fingers in front of his nose. "Penny for your thoughts."

"They're not worth that much," he said wryly, shaking his head. "*Kumme*, it's getting late. We'd better head back to the buggy now."

He scooted down the rock on his behind, and then reached for Eleanor's hand so she wouldn't slip on the boulder's icy sheen. *The last thing I need is to be responsible for anyone else getting hurt*, he thought ruefully.

Eleanor prattled all the way home and by the time Walker stopped on Pinewood Street to drop her off, his head was buzzing.

"*Denki* for a pleasant afternoon," she

said as she stepped down. "I'm looking forward to Wednesday evening."

Wednesday? Walker had been distracted through most of Eleanor's twaddle so he couldn't fathom what she was referring to until he was halfway down the street. *Ach! She must be going to the* Grischtdaag *program at the* schul, *too*, he realized with an ache in his stomach that rivaled the one in his head. *Oh well, at least talking isn't allowed from the audience during the presentation. Afterward, I'll just have to grab something to eat and make myself scarce.* Which was the same strategy he intended to employ when he got home in a few minutes, too.

Chapter Four

As uncomfortable as Fern was initially about spending the afternoon at the house Walker built for her cousin, once she got there her qualms diminished. Whether it was because it was located in a residential area and was much smaller than Fern expected it to be or because it seemed more like Louisa's home than Gloria's, whatever envy or bitterness Fern might have felt fell to the wayside. The house was just a house, and she grew increasingly relaxed being in it after Walker left.

It helped that the children were getting along so well, too. They spent nearly every minute of their visit with Jane outdoors running around or learning how to use her scooter. Patience took a spill and although her mittens and winter coat cushioned her hands and elbows, she scraped one of her knees and tore a hole in her long stockings. Fern was amazed Patience hadn't cried at all and she figured her daughter was doing her best to prove she could hold her own among the older kids. At home she usually pulled back when the other children were doing something physically challenging, so Fern was happy to notice this small change in her behavior.

Phillip, on the other hand, was his usual risk-taking self. With his hat abandoned and his coat unbuttoned, he sailed up and down the driveway on the scooter long after the girls decided to take a rest on the porch. He zipped back and forth so quickly Fern would have gone outside to warn him to slow down but he was as adroit as he was fast, maneuvering the scooter as easily as if it were an extension of his own body.

Meanwhile Fern enjoyed hearing updates about Serenity Ridge from Louisa, as well as news of Louisa's children, especially since Fern had gotten to know Walker's sister fairly well when she lived in Maine. In fact, Fern had first met Walker after Willa invited her to a quilting sister day at their house. Fern remembered how Walker had gotten in trouble with Louisa for helping himself to the peanut brittle Fern had brought before any of the women at the gathering had a chance to taste it.

Later, although he'd had plans to go bowling with some of the other single men in the district, his mother urged him to give Fern a ride home since it was raining and no one else was headed in her direction. Once they were courting, Walker confessed how disappointed he was because Fern had cut their conversation short that afternoon, asking to be dropped off several blocks from Roman's house.

She recalled feeling as if she could have talked to him all afternoon, too—a stark contrast with how she felt during today's buggy ride.

"It must be close quarters with seven *kinner* and three adults living together in a small *haus*, isn't it?" Louisa asked at one point.

"*Jah*, but we're used to it," Fern replied, forcing a bland smile.

She shied away from questions like these about her living situation. It wasn't that Walker's mother asked her anything especially private, but Fern assumed anything she said could be repeated and she didn't want Walker to know how much she'd struggled over the past couple of years. It was a matter of pride and pride was sinful but there were still certain topics—such as her financial challenges—Fern didn't wish to disclose.

She had hoped Louisa would serve the peanut butter cream pie in the late afternoon so she, Phillip and Patience could begin their long trek home before the daylight waned, but the children remained outside for so long the older woman said she'd serve the pie after their meal.

Fern hadn't planned on staying at Walker's home through supper, but Louisa's leftover roast beef, mashed potatoes and gravy were a welcome change from rice and beans. And now that Walker wasn't around, Fern's appetite was really kicking in, so she eagerly set the table while Louisa heated the food.

"Walker told me not to wait for him if he wasn't home by five, but let's add a plate just in case he shows up," she suggested.

Sure enough, just as everyone was settling into their chairs, they heard footsteps on the porch.

"Perfect timing, *suh.* Hurry and go wash your hands—we'll wait to say grace," Louisa instructed, causing Fern to wonder if she'd still be reminding Phillip to clean up for supper when he was Walker's age.

When he returned to the room, Walker

took the open seat at the foot of the table to Fern's left. "I'll pray," he volunteered.

Before everyone could bow their heads, Jane piped up, "Let's hold hands."

Fern and Phillip automatically joined hands but she hesitated before sliding her fingers onto Walker's open palm. As he gently curled his fingers around hers, she remembered all the times they'd sat knee to knee, hand in hand, praying about their relationship. It was through prayer that they'd come to believe they were God's intended for one another. *How could I have been so mistaken?* Fern wondered.

As everyone began passing serving bowls around the table, she once again felt too queasy to eat. Phillip, however, was clearly ravenous.

"*Suh*, there are five other people at the table," Fern said under her breath as the boy scooped himself a huge serving of mashed potatoes.

"There's plenty more where that came from," Louisa said with a wink at Phillip.

"As long as you eat what's on your plate, you can take as much as you like."

"Where did you go on your hike, *Daed*?" Jane questioned.

"Through the woods by Serenity Lake." Walker answered tersely, as if he didn't want to talk about it.

That's probably because he only left so he wouldn't have to be around me, Fern thought. Noticing he hadn't cracked a smile since he'd arrived, she figured he was disappointed to discover she, Phillip and Patience were still there. She hoped Louisa intended to bring them back to Roman's house so Walker wouldn't feel further inconvenienced about having to give them a ride.

"You went hiking alone? That doesn't sound like *schpass*," Jane commented.

Walker avoided a direct answer, replying, "I'm sure you three *kinner* had a lot more *schpass* being together, right?"

"*Jah*. We went horseback riding."

Walker's eyebrows jumped up. "On whose horse?"

"Not a real one—we were pretending the scooter was a horse. Phillip even let go of the reins with one hand."

"While your horse was trotting?" Walker asked Phillip, sounding impressed. Fern was surprised he was playing along; maybe she had misjudged his mood.

"*Neh*, it was running full speed," Phillip blustered, causing Fern to cover her smile with her napkin. "My *hut* flew right off but that's okay because my head usually gets too sweaty anyway."

"My head gets sweaty, too, especially when I have to wear a helmet for work," Walker commiserated. Then he asked Patience if she let go of the horse's reins with one hand, too.

"*Jah*, but I fell off," Patience admitted softly as she struggled to cut her meat with her fork. Walker reached over and sliced the roast beef for her.

"Did you get hurt?" he asked so compassionately, Fern's heart bloomed with unexpected fondness.

"My knee bleeded a little and I ripped my stockings," Patience answered. "*Mamm* will have to sew them because I'm not big enough to wear Emma's hand-me-down stockings yet."

Fern cringed at her daughter's revelation of just how poor they were, but Jane piped up, "You can have my hand-me-downs, can't she, *Groossmammi*?"

"I don't think Patience wants your old stockings, Jane," Walker interjected. "They *schtinke*."

"*Daed!*" Jane exclaimed. Then she addressed Patience, saying, "My stockings don't really *schtinke*. Not after *Groossmammi* washes them anyway."

Patience giggled and Louisa spoke up. "I actually think you have a few dresses you've outgrown. We can take a look in the trunk after supper. I may have stowed them away for quilting but it would be a much better use of the material if Patience could wear the dresses."

"I never get to hand down anything because all my littler *gschwischderkinner* are *buwe*," Jane explained sadly, as if she'd been cheated of an important privilege.

"That's too bad," Patience sympathized before turning to Fern. "Did you get to hand down your clothes to Jane's *mamm* when you lived together?"

"*Neh*. Gloria was taller than I was, even though she was younger. But one time she gave me a pretty lilac dress of hers. She took up the hem first."

"*Groossmammi* said my *mamm* didn't like to sew and she'd do anything to get out of it."

"That's true. But she took the hem up anyway as a surprise because she really wanted me to have the dress." Fern remembered this with affection. Gloria was as nearly as poor as Fern was, but she was always generous with whatever she had. Fern saw that same personality trait in her daughter, even if her mother had perished before Jane was old enough to copy her behaviors. *Maybe that characteristic is to Louisa's credit. Or to Walker's.* "Your *mamm* was very generous," she told Jane.

"What else was she like?"

Fern hesitated only briefly before singing Gloria's praises. In light of how kind Walker was being to her children, she knew she couldn't be stingy-hearted about Gloria in front of Jane, who understandably wanted to hear more about her mother from someone who'd known her well. "Your *mamm* was a very hard worker. And she looked just like you—she had the same deep brown eyes. She loved to sing and she had a very pretty voice."

"*I* love to sing. For the *Grischtdaag* program we learned lots of carols. I can sing one for—" Jane began to say but Walker cut her off.

"There's no singing at the table, remember?"

"We can sing it on the way to your *haus*," Jane promised Patience.

"I don't think you should ride with

them," Walker contradicted. "You need a bath before bedtime."

"Please?" Jane implored her grandmother, not her father. Fern noticed Louisa often had the final say in family matters and she wondered if it ever bothered Walker.

"It won't take very long to go to Roman's *haus* and back," Louisa reasoned, addressing her son. "If you leave right after dessert, there will be plenty of time for Jane to take a bath when you return."

If Walker was taken aback to be told he was giving Fern and the children a ride home, it didn't show on his face. He grinned at Phillip, suggesting he accompany him to hitch the horse, and the boy happily traipsed after him into the mudroom.

Meanwhile, Louisa went off in search of Jane's hand-me-downs and Fern and the girls cleared the table and rinsed the dishes. Just as they were finishing, Louisa returned with three dresses that she said she'd include in a bag full of ingredients for Fern's pantry since she knew the women in the district had completely emptied Roman's cupboards.

"You don't need to do that. We're walking to the store on Main Street tomorrow," Fern politely declined.

"It's supposed to rain tomorrow. Just take a few things so in case you don't go, you'll still be able to make fresh bread."

Fern was tickled to receive flour and fresh eggs, and she noticed the woman wrapped up the last piece of pie for Phillip, too. The children helped her carry the bags to the buggy, where Walker loaded the items into the back of the carriage. After tucking a blanket around the children, he unfolded one for Fern, too.

"Warm enough?" he asked after she'd spread it over her lap.

"Not yet," she used to answer when they were courting. He'd hand her a second blanket, inch closer to her on the seat and ask again. "*Neh*, not yet," she'd always reply. Then he'd slide close enough to wrap his arm around her from the side. "There," she'd say, snuggling against him. "*Now* I'm warm enough."

The memory brought heat to her cheeks and she couldn't help but wonder if Walker remembered it the minute the words were out of his mouth, too. She quickly answered, "*Jah*, I'm fine. *Denki*."

Then she began jabbering on about how her *Ordnung* in Ohio had recently begun allowing propane heaters in buggies but Adam didn't consider them safe, much to Linda's consternation, and the couple would have the same argument almost every Sunday they traveled to church, which was a terrible way to begin the Sabbath. Fern had no idea where she was headed with her story but fortunately, the children broke into a Christmas carol, which interrupted Fern's nonsensical ramblings and spared Walker from having to reply. The five of them sang all the way to Roman's house.

"*Denki* for bringing us back," she told him when he dropped them off. "You can feel free to use whatever tools you need from the barn tomorrow, of course. We'll probably be gone when you *kumme*."

At least, that's what Fern had planned, although it no longer seemed imperative to avoid the very sight of him. *I might not want to spend time alone with him, but with the* kinner *present, being in Walker's company is rather pleasant*, she thought.

In the morning, she woke to a hard rain hitting the windowpanes. Or was it sleet? In either case, Louisa had been right; the precipitation meant they wouldn't be walking into town that morning.

"Can Jane *kumme* to our *haus* to play?" Patience asked as she dug into her French toast at breakfast. They didn't have any syrup, but Fern had brought a small jar of strawberry jam in her purse to make sandwiches on the way from Ohio, so they spread that on the top of their French toast. It felt like such a treat.

Fern wished her daughter would stop referring to Roman's house as *their* house. "*Neh.* She has to go to *schul*, remember?"

"After she gets out she could *kumme* for supper," Phillip chimed in.

Fern appreciated how much her children wanted to spend more time with their cousin, but it would mean Walker would have to accompany Jane. Even if Fern was finding it easier to be around him, she was on such a strict grocery budget she doubted she'd be able to afford to buy meat from the store in town, and she couldn't imagine serving Walker the kind of meal she *could* afford, especially not after he'd worked up an appetite sawing and chopping wood all afternoon.

"*Neh.* If the rain stops, Jane's *daed* is going to be here chopping up the trees in the afternoons. So he'd have to go all the way to the *schul* and then *kumme* all the way back here with Jane. Then after supper he'd have to go all the way to their *haus*. I don't think he'd want to do that."

"I can ask him when he gets here," Phillip offered.

"*Neh!* You're not to talk to him about it," Fern snapped. She immediately felt bad and added, "But when he arrives, I'd appreciate it if you'd tell him he can use the stable so his *gaul* doesn't have to stand in the cold."

"Maybe I should ask him if he needs help with the tree, too," Phillip suggested.

"I don't know about that. He might be using dangerous equipment." Fern tousled her son's hair. "But once the sky clears, we'll all go outside and pick up branches from the other side of the *haus*. That will be very helpful."

But the rain kept up all morning, and by lunchtime Fern wondered if Walker would be coming at all. However, he showed up around one-thirty even though it was still drizzling. Since Phillip had to tell Walker about stabling the horse anyway, Fern allowed both him and Patience to go play outside for a while.

"Just stay away from Walker while he's working. If he's using a chain saw, he won't be able to hear you coming."

She watched through the window as Phillip ran to Walker's buggy wagon, the vehicle Amish men used to transport their larger equipment and supplies. Phillip was gesturing animatedly as he spoke, and watching him, Fern felt a pang of wistfulness. Phillip could hardly remember his own father, and he'd been asking a lot of questions about him lately. Fern wished he had a stronger male influence in his life. There was Adam, of course, but he had five children of his own and he worked such long hours he was rarely home as it was.

Fern sighed and ambled into the kitchen to make more bread—she intended to make eggs on toast for supper. She was glad they'd each had a good helping of broccoli the night before at Louisa's house, but Fern really needed to get to the store so they'd have more variety in their diet.

The revving of the chain saw disrupted her thoughts, and Fern set aside the bowl and wooden spoon to peek out the window and make sure the children weren't getting too close to Walker. But they were on the opposite side of the house, gathering branches and stacking them by the woodpile.

Marshall would have been pleased to see they're becoming so helpful, she mused. Once, when he realized it was only a matter of weeks before he succumbed to cancer, Marshall expressed concern about Phillip's future without him. "Patience has you to help her grow into womanhood, but who will Phillip have to teach him how to be a man?" he'd asked. "I hope you'll consider remarrying after I'm gone. Don't wait too long—a *bu* needs a *daed* to shape his character most when he's young."

He'd said it so matter-of-factly that Fern would have been appalled, but she knew that was how Marshall expressed himself. He was just being practical and he made a fair point, but Fern had no intention of marrying again. She'd married out of necessity once, but she wouldn't do it a second time, not even for her son's sake. *Maybe when I get back I could pair Phillip up with one of the men from* kurrich *and he could help with yard work or a carpentry project...*

Fern's mind wandered as she kneaded the bread dough. Then she molded it into a big round lump, plopped it in a bowl and draped a dishcloth over the top before setting it by the woodstove so it would rise nice and high. Wiping her hands on her apron, she discreetly peered out the window again—she didn't want Walker to think she was spying on him.

Fern noticed Patience was standing to the side of the house, her neck craned upward, but Phillip was nowhere in sight. She looked out the other window, but she still didn't see him, so she opened the door and walked to the end of the porch.

"Patience, where's your *bruder*?" she called.

Patience pointed to the large section of tree that had toppled and was wedged upside down between the ground and the trunk, forming a sharp incline. Fern gasped when she spotted Phillip, who had climbed halfway up the branch like a bear cub.

Flying across the yard in her stocking feet, Fern screamed, "Phillip, you stay right where you are!"

She needn't have worried; bent at the waist, the boy was frozen in a half-standing, half-crawling position. He gripped a small side limb with one hand and supported his torso with the other. His feet were planted against the trunk in such a way that his legs were extended straight up and his bottom stuck out.

"I'm stuck, *Mamm*," he said when she got closer. "The bark is too slippery for my boots. I can't move."

"Hold on, I'll *kumme* get you!" she

shouted as she pulled her socks from her feet so she'd have traction. As soon as she began scaling the broken tree, her skirt twisted around her legs. Trying to kick free, she lost her footing and would have fallen to the ground were it not for Walker's arms encircling her.

"Absatz!" he barked into her ear and set her upright on the frozen earth.

"Let me go!" She pushed his hands from her waist. "Can't you see my *suh* is in danger?"

"I do see," Walker said in a low voice despite the panic rising in his chest. "I also see this branch is in a very precarious position. Any more weight on it and it could split from the trunk. Phillip could get hurt and so could you."

They both eyed the young boy. His legs were beginning to shake from being fixed in the same position for so long. Sweat collected on the nape of Walker's neck. He shifted so he was standing beneath Phillip, who he estimated was about twelve feet from the ground.

"Roman must have a ladder in the barn. Go get it," Walker commanded Fern. He wasn't sure she could carry it herself, but he was positive if Phillip fell, she wouldn't be able to catch him, so Walker had to stay right where he was, posed to catch the boy himself if Phillip's endurance gave out.

"My legs are tired. I'm going to fall," Phillip whimpered.

"*Neh*, you aren't. You're a very strong *bu*. I noticed that about you right away," Walker told him, just as the tree creaked. The ladder was a bad idea—they couldn't put any more weight against the branch. Besides, with his body situated as it was, Phillip wouldn't be able to shift onto the ladder by himself.

"I've got it!" Fern yelled as she and Patience dragged the ladder across the frozen ground.

Phillip turned to look over his shoulder toward his mother.

"Don't look at your *mamm*—look down here at me!" Walker barked. "Listen to me and do just what I say. When I tell you, I want you to hold on tight with your hands and lower yourself onto your belly. You're going to walk your feet backward like this."

Walker crouched onto the ground below the branch and imitated the movements he wanted Phillip to copy. Then he said, "Once your belly touches the trunk, then you're going to wrap your legs around it. Okay, now."

Planting himself below the branch with his arms upstretched, Walker prayed, *Please, Lord, keep him from falling. Please, please, please don't let the branch break.*

"That's right," he encouraged the child as Phillip eased his feet backward until his stomach was almost resting on the trunk of the branch. His foot slipped and he instinctively wrapped his legs around the branch, which bounced from the force of the sudden shift of his weight. Walker continued to coax him. "That's *gut*. Now, you just hug that tree for a moment until you catch your breath." *And until I catch mine.*

"He's too heavy. It's going to break." Fern was at Walker's side trying to up-right the ladder. "We have to get him down from there."

Walker wrestled the ladder from Fern's arms and nearly knocked over Patience in the process. He didn't have time to explain. Through gritted teeth he com-manded her and Patience to clear the area before turning his attention to the boy again.

"Okay, Phillip, now I want you to swing your body around so you're hugging the tree from beneath the branch. I know you've probably let yourself down from a tree the same way before, right?"

"*Jah*, one time I did. But this tree's a lot higher."

"That's okay. I'm going to be standing

right under you so if you fall, I'll catch you."

Once the boy had maneuvered so he was twisted to the underside of the branch, Walker instructed him to dangle his legs. He had to work quickly, knowing the boy could lose his grip at any second. "You're being very brave. As soon as you dangle your legs, I'm going to count to three and then you're going to let go with your hands so I can catch you. Ready?"

Phillip followed his instructions perfectly and Walker managed to grab him right beneath his armpits, breaking his fall. The tree limb bounced upward and Walker yanked Phillip out of the way, just as the huge branch crashed down a couple yards to their left. Pieces of branches and bark flew up around them. Patience screamed and ran toward the house.

"Phillip!" Fern sobbed as she rushed to embrace her son.

"I'm okay, *Mamm*," he said, patting her back. "I'm okay."

In just that amount of time, all of Walker's concern and fear turned into irrepressible fury. "*Jah*, you are okay this time, but you could have been beneath that branch instead of standing here with your *mamm*!" Walker roared, pointing at the tree branch, his arm shaking. "Don't you ever, ever play by a cracked tree again, do you hear me?"

Phillip's lower lip trembled and his eyes welled, but Walker figured he'd rather the boy cry now than risk his life again in the future.

Fern released her son and pounced toward Walker like a lioness. "And don't *you* ever, ever yell at my *kind* like that again!" she warned, glaring up at him.

"Somebody has to—you obviously haven't taught him how dangerous it is to fool around on fallen trees!"

"Well, that somebody sure isn't *you*. You're not his *daed*!" Fern retorted. She shot him a final withering look, spun around and plucked her stockings from the ground where she'd shed them. She pulled Phillip with her as she made her way to the porch, where Patience was crouched on the steps with her head buried in her arms.

That's the thanks I get for rescuing her son? Fine! Leaving the ladder lying on its side, Walker wasn't going to stand around and be treated like that. He retrieved his chain saw and stormed toward the stable, where he piled his tools into the back of his buggy wagon, hitched the horse and then headed for home. His chest was so tight he felt as if it would burst open if he so much as inhaled, and there was a terrible racket in his ears, as if the chain saw were still abuzz. Halfway home he had to pull off to the side of the road because he got sick to his stomach.

He's okay, he told himself, wiping his mouth with the back of his hand. *Phillip's okay. He's not Jordan. He's okay.*

When he came through the door, his mother immediately questioned, "Why are you home so early? I thought you were going to work on the trees in Roman's yard."

"It's raining," he said, even though it was barely drizzling. "And I don't feel great. I'm going to take a shower." But afterward, Walker felt like he couldn't get warm again. He was still shivering as he set out to pick up Jane from school.

"Guess how many days until the *Grischtdaag* program?" she asked. "I'll give you a hint. It's less than three but more than one."

"Two," he said absently, pushing up his hat to rub his temple. Whatever Jane chattered on about for the rest of the ride, he didn't know. His mind was somewhere else; his mind was in the past. Despite all the times he'd prayed for the Lord to help him let it go, Walker feared the past would never be completely behind him.

He spent the rest of the afternoon in a daze, but he snapped to attention at supper time when Jane asked, "Can I invite

Phillip and Patience and Fern to *kumme* to the *Grischtdaag* program?"

"That's a lovely idea," Louisa agreed.

"Neh," Walker said at the same time.

"Why not?" Jane asked.

"You know better than to question an adult's decision. Now eat your green beans," Walker said firmly, pointing at Jane's plate.

His mother started to object but Walker scowled at her and she went silent. He appreciated how much help his mother had given him raising Jane, but sometimes he resented it that Louisa seemed to think her decision was the only one that counted. It was as if Walker were still as much of a child as Jane was.

After Jane was in bed, Louisa told him, "I need to go shopping tomorrow when you're done at the tree farm. If you pick me up on the way to Roman's *haus*, I'll ask Fern and the *kinner* if they'd like to go with me, since she likely didn't walk into town in the rain today."

"Fine." Walker preferred Fern and the kids weren't anywhere near him when he was working anyway.

However, avoiding them physically and avoiding thinking about them were two different matters, as Walker later discovered when he closed his eyes to sleep and images from the afternoon filled his mind. He'd put himself in harm's way to deliver Phillip from danger—and to keep Fern from experiencing the kind of sorrow Jordan's parents had suffered—and all she could do was berate him for scolding Phillip?

Amish parents frequently corrected each other's children as if they were their own, especially when they were jeopardizing themselves or someone else. Walker couldn't help but think if any other man had reprimanded Phillip after rescuing him, Fern wouldn't have flown off the handle the way she'd done today. Her words, "you're not his *daed*," echoed in Walker's mind. Her tone was so bitter it was almost as if she were blaming him for the fact her son's father died. Or maybe what she was really blaming him for—what she was really pointing out, once again—was that he'd married Gloria, not her.

Even though she doesn't know I never wanted to marry Gloria, isn't it time Fern got over her anger at me and moved on? Walker brooded. But considering how long he seethed into the night, he could have been asking himself the same question.

Chapter Five

Fern was so upset she hardly slept a wink. First, she was distressed because of the fright Phillip had given her. Second, she was livid because Walker had yelled at him and criticized her for being a bad mother. *Does he really think I'd allow my kinner to take unnecessary chances?*

That was a laugh—half the time, Fern fretted she was being *overly* protective of the children, especially of Phillip. And Walker was wrong if he thought she didn't admonish her children when they did something they shouldn't have done. But Fern hardly thought screaming at her son the instant after the branch practically came crashing down on his head was an appropriate way to handle the situation. So she waited until the following morning to discuss the incident with Phillip.

After breakfast she sat him down in the little front room and asked, "Do you remember what I told you about playing by the fallen tree?"

"*Jah.* You said not to play under it," Phillip somberly recited her instruction. "So I didn't. I only climbed on top of it."

Seeing his earnest expression, Fern realized he wasn't being cheeky—he had taken her directions to heart, word for word, and he guilelessly thought he'd obeyed them. It wasn't the first time. In Ohio, Fern recently had permitted the children to go outside after a rainstorm, but since she'd just scrubbed the kitchen floor she said they'd better not track even a speck of dirt into the house when they returned. Long after the rest of his cousins had come inside, Fern found her son on the porch, using his shirt hem to wipe the grooves of his boots. He was very literal-minded at this stage and he honestly tried his best to do what was asked of him. Fern couldn't fault him for that. She could only help him develop his comprehension.

"Why didn't I want you to play under the tree?" she asked, hoping to teach him to come to logical conclusions.

"Because the wind could blow it down on my head."

"*Jah.* Or it could have shifted on its own. If that happened and you were under it, you could have gotten crushed. But if you were on top of it, you could have fallen and broken your bones." Fern paused, giving him a chance to take in what she was telling him. "Next time I forbid you to play *under* something, I also mean don't play *on* it or anywhere *near* it. Otherwise, you could get hurt, and that would break my heart because you and your *schweschder* are the most precious things in my life."

Phillip nodded. "I'm sorry."

"It's okay. I know you won't do it again. But why did you climb it in the first place?" Fern was curious because Phillip rarely climbed trees at home, even though his cousins frequently did. He seemed to prefer speed over height and was more likely to spend his time outdoors hurdling fences and racing the goats.

Phillip studied his hands on his knees as he admitted, "Jane said the *Englischers* pay her *daed* to climb trees and cut their branches down. He doesn't just chop up the fallen parts."

His reply took Fern's breath away. *Phillip climbed the tree to impress Walker—to show Walker he could be like him!* In light of that realization, Fern grew even more incensed over how harshly Walker had reprimanded the child. It was one thing for Walker to crush *her* feelings the way he'd done, but for him to hurt her son's feelings was unconscionable. *What's wrong with him, losing his temper like that? Can't he see how much the* bu *looks up to him?*

Fern kissed Phillip's forehead and told him to scoot upstairs to make his bed, but she couldn't dismiss her acrimony toward Walker so easily, even though she prayed about it as often as the feelings of ill popped into her mind. *If there's any consolation in all of this it's that I recognize now more than ever what a mistake it would have been to marry him,* she thought. *Marshall wasn't perfect, but at least we saw eye to eye about how to raise the* kinner.

She planned to wait until right before Walker arrived to go to the store so she and the children wouldn't be at home while he was working in the yard. But after lunch Patience was so droopy she asked if she could lie down for a little while. To Fern's surprise, Phillip said he was tired, too, so both children crawled into their beds for a nap.

A few minutes later, Fern heard Walker's carriage pull into the yard. Rather than glancing out the window, she continued reading from her uncle's Bible until Walker knocked on the door. *He's probably here to offer an apology*, she thought. But since she didn't feel prepared to accept it, she dallied before opening the door.

She found Louisa, not Walker, standing on the doorstep. "Hello, Fern. I have to get groceries and I'm going to the superstore. Would you like to *kumme*?"

Fern bit her lip, hesitating. Although she'd prefer to limit her time with Walker's family, the superstore was so much cheaper than the market in town. "I'd appreciate that. The *kinner* are taking naps, but please *kumme* in and I'll get them up."

"*Neh*, don't wake them. I have time for a cup of tea first," Louisa said, even though she hadn't been offered one. Fortunately, Fern had four tea bags left over in her travel bag, which she surreptitiously retrieved while Louisa was using the bathroom.

After the water came to a boil, Fern poured the older woman and herself each a cup. "I'm sorry I don't have any honey. Do you take sugar?"

"Jah." Louisa dumped a heaping teaspoon into her cup and stirred the steaming liquid. "They say we're going to get a snowstorm this weekend. I hope it doesn't start up on *Samschdaag* before we leave for Willa's *haus* in Unity. She's expecting us for *Grischtdaag*."

"I hope it doesn't start on *Samschdaag*, either," Fern said. "We're scheduled to leave in the morning, too." *And I don't want anything to prevent us from going.*

"It's such a shame you can't stay longer. Jane loves being with her *gschwis-chderkinner* on Walker's side of the *familye*, but lately she's been curious about her *mamm*, especially since Roman died. Walker doesn't talk to her enough about Gloria, if you ask me. So it's been *wun-*

derbaar for her to meet you and to spend time with Phillip and Patience."

"They've enjoyed it, too," Fern murmured. What was Louisa expecting her to say? That she hoped they could get together again? Fern didn't plan on the children spending any more time together; she wanted to keep them as far away from Walker as possible.

But Louisa didn't broach the topic again. Instead, she rocked silently in the chair, frowning at the cup in her hands for so long Fern finally asked, "Is something wrong with the tea?"

"Oh, *neh*, dear. I'm sorry. I'm just so sleepy. Walker kept me awake last night. He was shouting in his sleep."

He did a lot of shouting during the day, too. "Did he have a nightmare?"

"I imagine so, but he clammed up when I broached the topic. Funny, but he hasn't had one that bad since…"

Despite how angry she was at Walker, Fern wanted Louisa to finish her sentence.

It sounded as if Walker suffered night-mares repeatedly. *Probably the sign of a guilty conscience.* "Since when?"

"Since right after the accident, when he was living at home still. I thought the terrors, as I call them, were from the concussion, but the doctors told me sometimes they can be a reaction to trauma," Louisa explained. "Which was understandable, considering his friend died right next to him. He was in such a dark mood for a long time afterward."

"Hmm," Fern murmured sympathetically, but she was thinking, *He wasn't so grieved that he postponed his wedding to Gloria.*

As if Louisa had read Fern's thoughts, she said, "I probably shouldn't be telling you this, but I pleaded with him not to marry Gloria—I didn't think he was in his right mind. But he was so insistent I began to think maybe marrying Gloria would help him. Instead, he seemed worse after that. She told me he had the terrors almost every night—they had to sleep in separate rooms for fear his thrashing would injure her or the *bobbel*. It wasn't until Jane was born that the nightmares subsided and Walker began to seem more like his old self again. Or at least not as depressed. I think becoming a *daed* helped him heal."

Fern swallowed. It wasn't easy hearing about how impatient Walker had been to marry Gloria, and there was no way Fern could chalk up that decision to his head injury because that would have been letting him off too lightly. She didn't relish hearing how happy it made Walker to have a baby with Gloria, either. But she understood why fatherhood would have changed his perspective, since having children had increased her joy, too.

"I haven't heard him yell out like that in his sleep during the entire time I've lived with him here, though." Louisa clucked her tongue against her teeth. "He's been so sullen these past couple of days, too. I don't know what's triggered it again after all this time."

Fern's hand trembled, causing her cup to rattle against its saucer. *She* knew what triggered Walker's terror: the incident with Phillip climbing the tree and the branch breaking. *That's* why Walker reacted as he did. He must have been reliving Jordan's accident. Fern should have known because being in the house where she'd tended to Roman had caused her to relive many upsetting memories, and they were minor compared to Walker's trauma.

"I think I know what's triggered it," she said softly. Then she described what had happened the previous afternoon, stopping short of telling her about how Walker had reacted afterward.

"Oh, that might explain it," Louisa acknowledged. "Walker works for the tree trimming company nine months out of the year, and being around falling limbs never seems to faze him. I guess the difference is that yesterday someone's safety was at stake. Maybe the situation with Phillip brought back memories of Jordan."

A shudder racked Fern's body as the full weight of Louisa's words sank in. *Walker wasn't* angry *at Phillip—he was* frightened *for him.* She glanced out the window. "He must be freezing out there. I think I'll take him a cup of tea before I wake the *kinner.*"

"*Gut.* That will give me a chance to take a little snooze," Louisa said, leaning her head back against the rocking chair.

Fern filled a mug and donned her coat, eager to apologize to Walker and to thank him for saving her son's life.

When Walker saw Fern coming toward him out of the corner of his eye, he reluctantly turned off the chain saw he'd borrowed from his employer. He expected her to chew him out again, but instead she smiled and extended a mug.

"It's warm."

"*Denki.*" He took a swallow.

"Sweet enough for your liking?" she asked, and for a moment he thought she was facetiously referring to her change in attitude. "Two sugars, right?"

Had she remembered that's how he took his tea or had his mother prepared it for him? Knowing Louisa, she'd probably *ordered* Fern to bring it to him, too. *"Jah."*

"Gut. Because after my behavior yesterday, I figured you probably need something warm and sweet," she said, dipping her head and tapping at the frozen ground with the toe of her boot.

What brought this on all of a sudden? Now Walker *really* suspected his mother's interference.

"Listen, I'm sorry for getting so angry at you for yelling at Phillip," she apologized. "I realize now how frightening it must have been to see him in a potentially perilous situation like that considering... you know, your accident."

So *that* was it. His mother heard him shouting in his sleep the night before and she told Fern about his nightmares. But Walker didn't need Fern's sympathy—he needed her to appreciate what a foolish thing her son had done by climbing the broken section of the tree.

"Yelling at Phillip had nothing to do with Jor—with the accident. I wasn't frightened—I was angry," he firmly informed her. "He shouldn't have been climbing the tree and quite frankly, I blame you for that. You should have warned the *kinner* to keep away from it the minute you came to stay here."

"I *did* warn them to keep away from it!" Fern protested, her eyes flashing.

"So he was deliberately being disobedient? Then he probably needs a man to teach him how to make better choices instead of just having his *mamm* coddling him after he's misbehaved."

"That's true. He does need a man to teach him. Not to intimidate or holler at him, but to *teach* him," Fern retorted. "Unfortunately, his *daed* is dead, so he's left with me. I'm doing my best..." Her eyes were brimming and Walker felt terrible, knowing his words had brought her to the brink of tears. She took a deep breath before continuing, "Phillip climbed the tree because he wanted to impress you, Walker. Don't ask me why, but for some reason, he admires you."

She spun on her heel to leave but Walker swiftly reached for her arm. "*Neh*, wait. Don't go." She wouldn't turn to face him but she stopped walking. "You're right. I overreacted. Wh-what happened with Phillip did remind me of—of the accident. I lost my temper at him because I'd never want another *elder* to suffer the way Jordan's *eldre* suffered after they lost their *suh*."

Now Fern twisted around, her slate-gray eyes still watery as she searched his face. "You've suffered deeply, too, haven't you, Walker?"

Jah, but not only because Jordan lost his life—but because I lost the life I dreamed of having, too. His voice was barely audible when he replied, "Not nearly as much as his *familye*."

"You've still suffered."

"The Lord has healed much of my sorrow."

"But it still grips you sometimes, when you least expect it, doesn't it?"

What else had his mother been telling her? Walker took a step backward. "How do you know that?"

"From being with people I care about who were ill. Who were dying." Fern shivered. She paused before changing the subject. "I'm sorry for not thanking you for rescuing Phillip yesterday. I don't want to think about what would have happened if I had climbed the tree or used the ladder to try to get him down myself."

I don't want to think about that, either. Walker's voice trembled as he expressed contrition, too. "I'm sorry for criticizing you as a parent. From the little bit I've witnessed, I can see what an excellent *mamm* you are, although I appreciate how difficult it must be raising the *kinner* on your own."

"I'm not really raising them on my own—Adam and Linda help."

Remembering all Fern had done for her relatives, Walker doubted Adam and his wife were as much of a help to Fern as she was to them. "My *mamm* helps me, too, but sometimes, I could use a little *less* help, if you know what I mean," he joked about his mother's bossiness.

Fern giggled impishly. It was the first time since she'd been back that Walker had heard her laugh, and he hoped it wouldn't be the last. "Speaking of your *mamm*, I should get inside now. The *kinner* are probably up from their naps, and Louisa is taking us shopping."

"Okay," he said, although he regretted their conversation drawing to a close. He handed her back the mug, wryly thinking, Jah, *that was* definitely *warm and sweet enough for my liking.* And by that, he didn't mean the tea.

Inside the house, Fern found Louisa helping Patience button her coat as Phillip was pulling on his boots.

"Did you have a *gut* rest?" she asked.

"Jah," Louisa answered. Fern smiled; she'd actually been asking the children, but she was glad to hear Walker's mother had had a refreshing catnap, too.

When they got outside, Walker approached. "Hi, *kinner,*" he said cordially, as if nothing ever happened the day before. While Phillip returned Walker's greeting, Fern noticed the boy averted his eyes until Walker asked, "Hey, Phillip, instead of going shopping with the women, can you give me a hand here? I can't cut wood and stack it, too."

Phillip puffed up his chest. "I can stay here, can't I, *Mamm*? Walker needs me."

"Jah. Just steer clear of the saw and do whatever Walker tells you to do." Filled

with gratitude for Walker's kindness, Fern caught his eye and mouthed the word *denki*. When he winked in return, she felt her cheeks burning all the way to the superstore.

Once there, she and Patience separated from Louisa, agreeing to meet back at the buggy when they were done shopping. Fern placed a small ham in her cart, as well as milk, oatmeal and frozen vegetables. She would have preferred to buy fresh produce, but frozen was cheaper and she wanted to have enough money to bake a dessert to have on hand in case Jaala and her grandchildren came by. Or to offer Walker. *In case he needs sustenance while he's doing all that work outside*, she told herself.

Snickerdoodles were easy and inexpensive, but since there was a sale on peanuts, she decided to make peanut brittle instead, since the children had never tasted it. After collecting the necessary ingredients, as well as a few more staples, Fern estimated her total bill. Thanks to the meals and pantry items Louisa had shared, Fern figured she had enough money left over to purchase a warm pair of stockings for Patience, so they swung by the clothing department before checking out.

Louisa took longer to shop than Fern did, so by the time the older woman circled back to the buggy, it was so late they had to go directly to the school to get Jane. Patience, who was usually such a wallflower in new surroundings, surprised Fern by asking if she could wait on the stairs for her cousin to come outside. She balanced on the bottom step, hugging the newel post until the doors opened and the children flooded out. Then she moved off to the side until Jane came trudging down the stairs. Although Fern couldn't hear their conversation, she could tell by the big hug Jane gave Patience that she was tickled to see her there.

"Hi, *Groossmammi*, hi, Fern," she greeted them when the girls climbed into the buggy. "I thought *Daed* was going to pick me up."

"Isn't it nice that we've *kumme* instead?" Louisa prompted.

"*Jah*. It's *schpass* to be with just *meed* for a change," Jane chirped from the back seat.

"Your *daed* and Phillip are probably at home saying how much *schpass* it is *not* to be with just *meed* for a change," Fern joked.

"They might think so, but they don't get to eat *kuchen* like we do," Louisa said. Then she instructed her granddaughter to open the package of shortbread cookies and pass them around. "Don't tell. It's our little secret."

"What is?" Fern teased. "That we're eating *kuchen* before supper or that you bought the *kuchen* instead of made them yourself?"

"Both," Louisa said with a hearty laugh, and Fern was pleased her fretful mood had lifted.

When they got back to the house, Louisa went inside to warm up, and Jane and Patience carried Fern's groceries to the porch so Fern could check in on Walker and Phillip.

"Wow, you've made some *gut* progress here," Fern complimented them. Phillip's cheeks were ruddy but he didn't stop piling small logs into the wheelbarrow.

"That's because many hands make light work," Walker said. "Or even an extra pair of hands makes light work when the hands are as capable as Phillip's."

The girls ran up at that moment, calling, "Hi, Phillip!"

"Hi," he said over his shoulder as he tossed another log into the wheelbarrow.

"Do you want to go race down the hill with us?" Jane asked.

"*Neh*, I'm working."

"Actually, Phillip, I think we're done for the day. You can go play with the *meed*," Walker suggested.

Phillip lifted his hat to wipe his brow.

"You sure you can manage wheeling this load over to the woodpile by yourself?"

Walker bit his lip and Fern stifled a chuckle, too. "I think I can handle it. *Denki* for all your help today."

"You're welcome. I'll meet you here the same time tomorrow," Phillip said as if he were Walker's hired hand. Then he was a young boy again, darting off and challenging the girls to beat him to the top of the hill.

"*Denki* for letting him stay with you. He really hates shopping," Fern said.

"No thanks needed—he was a huge help," Walker said, tossing a wood chip onto the tarp he'd spread nearby. "But I understand why he hates shopping. Especially at this time of *yaahr*. I can't stand it, either."

"Really? You never let on when I'd ask you to take me shopping. Remember that year I couldn't decide whether to get Gloria a stationery set or a glass pie plate for her birthday? You must have taken me to five different *Englisch* stores. You were so patient."

Walker's smooth mustache broadened with his grin. "How could I forget? After going back and forth and back and forth, you bought her teacups instead. Didn't they have flowers on them?"

"Tulips, *jah*."

The china was as beautiful as it was impractical, and Fern could only afford to purchase two cups and saucers. Gloria kept them hidden away in her bedroom because she said she didn't want her father to accidentally break them, although Fern suspected what she really feared was that Roman would consider the decorative pattern too "worldly." On special occasions after he went to bed, Gloria would take them out, and the girls would sneak upstairs so they could chat and drink tea in the elegant cups in private.

Thinking about it, Fern felt a hollow achiness deep inside. Despite what Gloria had done, Fern had loved her cousin.

And she realized if she missed Gloria, Walker must have missed her three times as much. Feeling ashamed she'd withheld her condolences for this long, Fern uttered, "I loved Gloria deeply and I know you must have loved her even more. I'm sorry she's gone."

Walker's green eyes dimmed and his mouth settled into a straight line in such a way he almost looked angry instead of sad. In a low tone he said, "*Denki*. And I'm sorry you lost your spouse—sorry that Marshall died, I mean."

"*Denki*," Fern replied simply.

There was something about directly acknowledging Gloria's death that made Fern feel as if she'd taken a step closer to…well, not to reconciling the past, necessarily, but to being a little more at peace with it. And maybe even with Walker.

Fern headed inside and Walker delivered the final load of logs to the woodpile, reflecting on the exchange they'd just shared, as well as on their conversation from earlier that afternoon. As he considered Fern's comments, he realized he'd been underestimating her capacity for empathy, not only toward her cousin, but also in regard to how the accident had affected Walker.

If she can be that understanding of me, I can definitely be more charitable about Jane inviting her gschwischderkinner *to the* Grischtdaag *program*, he thought. *Especially now that Fern and I are getting along better.*

So, after he'd stowed the chain saw and wheelbarrow in the barn, Walker called loudly in the direction of the backyard, "Jane! *Kumme* here!" All three children came scampering from around the house.

"Do we have to go already?" Jane whined. "I just got here."

"*Jah*, but you can see Phillip and Patience again tomorrow night."

"*Neh*, I can't. Did you forget about the

Grischtdaag program, *Daed*? It's tomorrow after supper."

"Ah, so it is." Walker scratched the hair on his chin. "Then I suppose you'll just have to invite them to the program."

The whites of Jane's eyes went as large as eggs. "But you said—"

Walker put a finger to his lips to shush her before saying, "Provided their *mamm* says *jah*, they can *kumme*."

"Let's go ask her. I'll race you!" Phillip was off like a shot with Jane close behind him, but Patience hung back, clearly tuckered out.

"I don't want to race, either," Walker said, slowing his pace so she could keep up with him.

After a few yards, she remarked, "*Mamm* says you know a whole bunch about trees."

Really? That was complimentary of her. "Maybe not a whole bunch, but I know a few things. Why—is there something you want to ask me about them?"

Instead of posing her question directly, Patience told him, "*Mamm* says if there was another tree in the yard that was going to fall, you would have seen it and chopped it down before we got here. She says it's only a little branch hitting my ceiling at night but that doesn't mean the whole tree is going to tip over."

Ah, now Walker understood. He stopped and pivoted in the direction of the tree nearest the house. After studying it thoughtfully, he said, "Your *mamm* is right. That's a very sturdy, healthy tree. It's just sort of waving its limbs around in the wind, kind of like you do when you're really happy to see someone or you want to get their attention. And it's so close to the roof, it taps against it, that's all. But if it keeps you awake at night, I can cut the branch down tomorrow." He began moving toward the house again.

"How?" Patience asked, slipping her hand into his and trotting alongside him just like Jane would have done.

"I'll use a tool called a pole saw."

"Will you have to climb the tree?"

"I'll go up on a ladder, *jah*."

Patience fiercely shook her head. "*Neh*, that's okay. I don't care anymore if it taps my ceiling."

It occurred to him that Patience didn't want him to go up in the tree because she was traumatized by Phillip's near accident the previous day, too. *If I'm going to climb any ladders or trees, I'd better not do it in her presence*, Walker decided as he and Patience caught up to Jane and Phillip on the porch.

"Look, *Daed*—they lit candles in the windows!" Jane exclaimed.

"The *haus* has never looked so pretty, has it?" Walker remarked. Roman didn't permit Christmas decorations; he thought they were too showy. It always disappointed Jane, just as it had disappointed Gloria before her.

Before he could rap on the door to let his

mother know he was ready to leave when she was, Louisa and Fern stepped outside.

"Can we go to the *Grischtdaag* program tomorrow night, *Mamm*?" Phillip asked, hopping from foot to foot. "Jane invited us."

Fern hedged, "We don't have a way to get there and it will be dark—"

Louisa interrupted, "When he's done working here, Walker could bring you with him to pick up Jane from *schul* and then circle around to our house. We'd all eat supper and then we'd go to the *schul* together. Walker will bring you home, too."

Walker got the sense his mother had hatched this scheme even after he'd told Jane she couldn't invite Patience, Phillip and Fern to the program. But instead of feeling chagrined that she must have suspected he'd change his mind, Walker was glad she'd come up with the idea.

"*Denki*, that would be *wunderbaar*," Fern said. "Wouldn't it, *kinner*?"

"*Jah!*" they chorused, jumping up and down.

Walker's heart leaped, too, much like it had the very first time Fern accepted an invitation to spend an evening out with him.

Chapter Six

Fern was glad she'd purchased ingredients to make peanut brittle because now she'd have a treat to bring to the Christmas program to share with the other families. She also told Louisa she'd make scalloped potatoes with ham for supper. Louisa tried to object but Fern insisted, so the older woman said she'd prepare stewed tomatoes and green beans to go with the potatoes and ham. Which meant the meal would help compensate for the vegetables the children had been missing in their diet.

As Fern took a mixing bowl from the

cupboard on Wednesday after they'd eaten an early lunch, Patience asked, "Can I help you bake, *Mamm*?"

"I'd appreciate that," she answered. "Do you want to help, too, Phillip? There are lots of potatoes to peel."

"*Neh*. I want to move the logs we didn't get to yesterday," he said as pushed one arm through his coat sleeve.

"Aren't you going to wait for Walker to get here?"

"*Neh*. The more I do now, the less Walker will have to do on his own once I leave," Phillip replied seriously.

As he headed out the door, Fern noticed he wasn't wearing his hat again, but she didn't remind him. He was right when he said it made his head sweat, and Fern was more concerned about him running around with wet hair than with cold ears.

"I wish I could be in a *Grischtdaag* program," Patience said a few minutes later as she spread butter around on a cookie sheet to keep the peanut brittle from sticking to it.

Patience was usually so bashful she wouldn't speak in front of a group of her peers, much less in front of an audience of strangers. There was something about her being with Jane that emboldened her in a way being around Emma didn't. Fern sensed it was that Jane was more tolerant, more encouraging, whereas Emma understandably tired of Patience shadowing her.

"Well, you'll get to be in one when you go to *schul*."

"I wish we could stay here and I could go to *schul* with Jane."

"What about your *gschwischderkinner* in Ohio? Don't you want to go to *schul* with them?" Going to school with her cousins was something Patience had been anticipating ever since Emma started school.

"Jah," Patience answered. "But they have lots of *kinner* in their *familye*. Jane doesn't have a *schwesder*. Or a *bruder*. So

she'd probably like it if Phillip and I went to *schul* with her."

Fern was touched that Patience was concerned Jane might have been lonely. At the same time, she had to keep her daughter's hopes about remaining in Serenity Ridge in check. "That's true. If we lived here, Jane would love going to *schul* with you and your *bruder.* We have to leave on *Samschdaag,* but I know Jane is very *hallich* you get to visit her *schul* tonight."

Patience held up the cookie sheet so Fern could make sure she hadn't missed buttering any spots. Fern pointed to a corner and Patience traced it with the stick of butter, asking, "*Mamm,* why don't you want to live here?"

"It's not that I don't want to…" Actually, it was. Fern started again. "We already have a home in Ohio."

"That's *Onkel* Adam and *Ant* Linda's home, not ours. Emma said so."

Fern tried not to let her annoyance come through in her tone. "Everything anyone has comes from the Lord. He's the One who gives us a *haus* to live in and a *kuh* for *millich* to drink and a *gaarde* of food to eat. All those things are His, but He shares them with us because He's so generous. So you see, the *haus* in Ohio belongs to *Gott* even more than it belongs to your *onkel* or *ant*. Or to Emma. *Gott* is just letting them use it for now. And they're sharing it with us."

Patience was quiet. After she finished buttering the corner of the cookie sheet, she set it flat on the table and asked, "Does this *haus* belong to *Gott*, too?"

"*Jah.*" Fern smiled brightly, pleased her daughter understood her point. "It does."

"Then I'm going to pray and ask *Gott* if He'll let us live in it."

Inwardly, Fern groaned. She hadn't told her children anything about the inheritance or her plan to sell Roman's house and get a place of their own in Ohio. For one thing, it wasn't appropriate to include them in adult matters; for another, she didn't want them to get too excited too early in case her plans went awry. However, she was beginning to think it might be a good idea to tell them sooner rather than later. *Maybe I'll tell them at* Grischtdaag, *sort of as a gift.*

For the moment, she said, "Patience, all of our relatives are back in Ohio."

"Not all of them. Jane isn't." Patience was being unusually assertive. "Walker isn't."

"Walker isn't your relative." Technically, he *was* related, but only by marriage, and for some reason, the distinction was important to Fern.

"But if we lived here, maybe he'd ask you to marry him and then he'd be my *daed.*"

"Patience!" Fern yapped, slapping her mixing bowl down on the table. "I don't want to hear you talking nonsense like that again, do you hear me?"

Patience's nose went pink, like it did when she was cold, and her eyes simultaneously filled with tears. *"Jah, Mamm,"* she rasped. Then she fled the room, and the pattering of her footsteps as she scurried up the stairs tattered Fern's heart. Nothing hurt a mother more than causing her own children pain.

Why did I react so strongly? she reproached herself. *Am I really so worried she'll tell Jane about her absurd wish that Walker will marry me?* Even if she did and Jane repeated it to her father, Walker undoubtedly would have recognized it as being a child's fantasy, not an idea that originated with Fern.

Disgusted at herself for being overly sensitive, Fern washed her hands and dried them on her apron before climbing the stairs. She expected to find Patience curled up on the bed, but instead she was standing at the window, her back to the door. Although Fern couldn't hear her, she could tell by the way her daughter's shoulders were moving up and down that Patience was sobbing.

Fern sat on the bed. "Patience, *kumme* here. Please *kumme* sit with your *mamm*."

Hanging her head, Patience edged toward her, stopping a couple of feet shy of her mother. Fern reached out to pull the girl onto her lap and cuddled her to her chest, the way she did when she was an infant. Whereas Phillip was always on the move—his restlessness even kept Fern awake during her pregnancy with him—Patience always liked being rocked. *How much longer will she let me hold her like this?*

"I'm sorry for snapping at you," she murmured into her daughter's fine hair. "I didn't mean to be so crabby."

Fern hummed, rocking a few minutes more before Patience pulled her head back to ask, "Don't you like Walker, *Mamm*?"

"*Jah*, he's our friend and he's been very helpful to us," Fern answered diplomatically. "But two people need to *love* each other in a special way in order to get married."

Patience seemed to think this over before questioning, "Can I still ask *Gott* if we can live in this *haus*?"

"You can ask, but *Gott* might have another *haus* for us to live in. One that's in Ohio, close to *Onkel* Adam and his *familye*," Fern cautioned, planting the possibility in Patience's mind. "Now, we'd better get downstairs and finish making that peanut brittle or we won't have anything to share at the *Grischtdaag* program."

"Can I wear the dress Jane gave me tonight?"

Fern tapped her daughter's nose. "If we finish baking lickety-split so I can take in the seams."

By the time Phillip came in, the peanut brittle was beginning to cool and Fern had peeled and sliced all the potatoes. After guzzling down a glass of water, he remarked, "Walker will be *hallich* to see how many more logs I piled into the wheelbarrow."

It occurred to Fern that Phillip was becoming as fond of Walker as Patience was of Jane. *I'm glad they're forming a connection but I hope they don't get* too *close to their* gschwischderkind *or to Walker,* she worried. *Because if they do, no one knows as well as I do how difficult it will be for them to leave Serenity Ridge.*

Walker had reason to whistle on his way to Roman's house. For one thing, he'd slept through the night without stirring even once. For another, the customers he interacted with at Swarey's Christmas Tree Farm had been in such cheery moods it was contagious. Most importantly, his daughter's greatly anticipated Christmas program that evening was going to be all the more meaningful to her because Phillip, Patience and Fern would be in attendance—and there were few things in life that made Walker as joyful as witnessing Jane's delight.

When he arrived at Roman's house, Phillip was waving from the porch. Walker noticed the rest of the wood they hadn't collected yesterday was now stacked high in the wheelbarrow.

"Did you stack all those logs yourself or did you have a team of men helping you?" Walker asked once he'd unhitched and stabled the horse.

"*Neh*. I did it alone," Phillip answered, as if Walker sincerely suspected otherwise. "But I couldn't move the wheelbarrow myself. It's too heavy."

"Looks like it's pretty full. It might be too heavy for me, too."

"I could lift one handle and you could take the other side," Phillip suggested, but Walker figured they'd end up tipping the barrow, so he said he'd give it a try first.

After wheeling the logs to the woodpile, he told Phillip he had a very important job for him—holding the ladder while Walker ascended it. Before Walker began cutting up the smaller of the two trees that had been damaged, he wanted to trim the branch that was knocking against the roof above Patience's bedroom. Since she was indoors, this was an opportune time for him to do it without her seeing him.

They retrieved the ladder from the barn and Walker's pole saw and two helmets from his buggy. "I doubt any branches will drop on our heads, but it's better to be safe than sorry," he told Phillip as he tightened the helmet strap beneath the boy's chin.

It only took a couple of minutes for him to saw through the small branch, and after Walker descended the ladder, he said, "*Gut* job. You've got a firm grip."

"I'm going to work construction like my *daed*," Phillip told him. "Or maybe I'll be a tree cutter, like you."

Over the years, Walker had occasionally imagined what it would be like to have a son to follow in his footsteps, but because he wasn't ever going to marry again, he'd trained himself to disregard the daydream as soon as it sprang to mind. However, working with Phillip gave Walker a glimpse of what he might have been missing, so he relished the opportunity to mentor the boy, if only for a few days.

The pair worked for nearly an hour and a half before Fern appeared on the front porch. She cupped her hands to her mouth and called, "Would either of you like a snack?"

Phillip answered for both of them. "*Jah,* we would!"

Walker trailed him into the house. They both took their shoes off at the door before following the mouth-watering aroma into the kitchen.

"We sure worked up an appetite," Phillip announced, and from the twinkle in Fern's eye, Walker could tell she found the child's adult mannerisms as amusing as Walker did.

"The potatoes and ham you smell are for later, but sit down and have some peanut brittle and *millich* to tide you over until supper."

"Peanut brittle?" Walker repeated. He

pulled out a chair and seated himself next to Phillip as Patience tiptoed toward him, carefully balancing a small plate heaped with candy. He told her, "It looks and smells *appenditlich*. Your *mamm* always made the best peanut brittle in Serenity Ridge."

"*Denki*," Fern mumbled. "But I didn't make this myself. Patience helped."

"The piece on top is for you," Patience told him, holding the plate beneath his nose. "You get the biggest one because you cut down the branch above my window."

He smiled at the little girl as he selected the treat she'd indicated was his. "You saw me doing that?"

"Only for a little bit, and then I went into the kitchen with *Mamm*. She couldn't watch because it made her nerves afraid, too," Patience explained as she offered the plate of peanut brittle to Phillip.

Fern's nerves were frayed? Walker realized plenty of people were afraid of heights and he shouldn't take it personally that watching him had made Fern nervous, yet he was still touched by her concern for his safety. "I was fine. Phillip was holding the ladder nice and steady for me."

"That's because I'm getting practice for when I go to work," Phillip said, accepting a glass of milk from Fern. She set a glass in front of Jane and Walker, too, and then took a seat at the table across from him.

"Mind your teeth," she warned the children. "Peanut brittle is crunchy."

The four of them bit into their candy at the same time and Walker gave a contented moan when he tasted the buttery richness of the dessert. He took another bite and when he finished chewing, he told Patience in a magnified whisper, "Don't tell your *mamm* I said so, but this peanut brittle is even better than when she used to make it by herself."

Patience gave a self-conscious smile and leaned over to confide, "That's because we did something secret when we were making it."

"Did you add a pinch of love?" Walker guessed. He quoted a cliché Fern used to say: "Everything tastes better when it's made with love."

Phillip snorted. "That's *lappich*."

But Patience scrunched her eyebrows together in thoughtful consideration. *"Neh,"* she replied slowly. "If you put love in something you bake, it would melt."

It took every ounce of Walker's willpower not to crack up and Fern was covering her mouth, too.

Patience, fortunately, was oblivious. She took a swallow of milk before revealing, "The secret is you have to warm the cookie sheets first because that gives you extra time to spread the mixture on them."

"Aha!" Phillip pointed at her. "You just said what the secret was. It's not a secret anymore." Patience's shoulders drooped as her brother laughed; it was the only time Walker had seen any hint of discord between them.

"That's okay," Fern comforted Patience instead of scolding Phillip for taunting her. "Most people are *schmaert* enough to know if they tell a woman's cooking secrets or criticize her baking, she'll probably serve them the smallest piece of dessert the next time she makes it."

"That's right," Walker confirmed, patting Patience's head. Then he ribbed Fern, "You *did* hear me say how *appenditlich* your peanut brittle is, didn't you?"

She rolled her eyes, but her riposte was playful. "Most people also know that flattery will get them nowhere. But if you want more, please help yourself, Walker."

"*Denki,*" he said with a smug grin, reaching for the candy.

"What's flattery?" Phillip asked.

"It's when someone says something nice to you that they don't really mean."

"But I *did* mean what I said about your peanut brittle being the best in Serenity

Ridge," Walker insisted. *I meant every word of everything I ever said to you.* With more seriousness than the conversation warranted, he looked directly at Fern and reiterated, "It wasn't flattery. It was the truth. I wouldn't tell you something unless I meant it."

In this light, Fern's eyes were pearly gray and as she returned Walker's unblinking stare with an intense gaze of her own, it seemed she understood he was no longer discussing candy. "I believe you," she said, her voice barely audible.

She believes what? *That I wasn't lying about the peanut brittle or that I wasn't lying about how much I loved her?*

"*Kumme.*" Phillip tugged on Walker's sleeve. "We still have work to do outside, right, Walker?"

"Right," he answered, rising quickly. He wasn't sure what had just transpired between Fern and him, but whatever it was had taken his breath away. He needed fresh air and he needed it fast.

* * *

Because Patience volunteered to pick up stray wood chips and other debris near the fallen tree, Fern was left alone to finish hemming the dress from Jane. She was glad for the solitude, which allowed her to ponder Walker's reaction to her teasing. *He sure got awfully serious all of a sudden*, she thought. *It was as if I'd personally maligned his character just because I suggested he was flattering me about the peanut brittle.*

But deep down, Fern wondered if Walker's vehement response had less to do with food than with his feelings. When he said, "I wouldn't tell you something unless I meant it," could he have been referring to his past declarations of love for her?

As Fern deftly worked the needle in and out of the fabric, her thoughts continued to drift. What if Louisa was right, and Walker only married Gloria as a result of the trauma? It was possible his near-death experience had given him a sense of urgency about moving forward with his life. Maybe Walker had decided he couldn't wait for Fern to come back—that he wanted to be married and have a child as soon as possible, lest something else happen before he had the opportunity.

Suppose that's the case. What does it really change anyway? she asked herself. Even without understanding the reasons behind Walker's decision to marry Gloria, Fern had already come to a truce with him. What more did she need to know? The past was over and by this time next week, she'd be back in Ohio, hopefully researching new places to live. *How exciting that will be!* she mused, setting her mending aside.

Before calling the children inside to get ready for their outing, she took advantage of her time alone to wash her face, comb her hair and put on her good church dress without any interruptions. Then, as the children cleaned up and changed their clothes, she transferred the potatoes and peanut brittle into portable containers. Walker pulled up in front of the house just as Fern and the children opened the door.

"For me? You shouldn't have," he joked, taking the containers so she could climb into the buggy unencumbered.

Fern giggled, glad to put the strangeness of their earlier interaction behind them. Once everyone was seated and the buggy was rolling down the street, she began pointing out landmarks to her children, who leaned forward to look out the front window.

"That road leads past the ice cream shop I told you about," she said over her shoulder.

"You mean Brubaker's?" Walker asked.

"Jah."

"It's not there anymore. They moved back to Ontario the summer after you left."

"Really? That's a shame."

"It's okay, *Mamm.* Jane will show us a

different ice cream shop this summer," Patience consoled her.

"This summer?" Walker sounded perplexed.

Fern surreptitiously tapped his arm and put a finger to her mouth, shaking her head. She didn't want to ruin the festive mood by reminding Patience they wouldn't be in Maine in the summer. In a voice loud enough for the children to hear, she asked him, "Where do people go to get ice cream cones in Serenity Ridge now?"

"We go to Foster's. They still have a shop on Lincoln Avenue."

Fern was familiar with the *Englisch* creamery, but she'd never been there herself. "Do they have cotton candy ice cream?"

"I don't think so."

"That's too bad. Cotton candy was Gloria's favorite flavor." Fern was surprised by how natural it felt to mention Gloria now. A little farther down the road, she told the children, "There's the street that leads to the library. Walker used to pick me up there when—"

Fern cut her sentence short, mortified she'd almost disclosed that Walker used to pick her up at the library when they were courting. They'd chosen that location because Roman never visited the library, so there was virtually no chance of him traveling down the small side road during the day. Fern's uncle was usually asleep by the time Walker brought Fern home, but Walker would drop her off at the end of the street by her house, just to be on the safe side.

Ever attentive to the smallest nuance, Patience asked, "When *what, Mamm?*"

"When it was raining and I needed a ride to visit our friends," Fern said. She quickly added, "He'd give Gloria a ride, too." Fern silently prayed Walker wouldn't elaborate on her response, which was technically true but shamefully misleading. Walker *had* picked Fern up in the rain. Occasionally Gloria accompanied them, too, and they continued on to attend singings with the rest of the youth in Serenity Ridge. However, more often than not when Walker picked Fern up, it wasn't raining and they were headed off to go hiking or out to supper alone, not with Gloria or anyone else. But Fern had never told the children that Walker had courted her before marrying Gloria, and she didn't want them to ever find out.

Patience was still puzzled. "Why didn't he pick you and Gloria up at *Onkel* Roman's *haus*?"

Fern's mouth went dry. To her relief, Walker replied, "Because the library was halfway between our *heiser* and both Gloria and your *mamm* loved to read. So they'd take the shortcut through the woods and read while they were waiting for me to *kumme* get them."

His answer relieved Fern and satisfied Patience, who sighed and said, "*I* love to read, too."

"*I* love to explore the woods," Phillip piped up. "Will you show us the shortcut tomorrow, *Mamm*?"

"Maybe. It depends on the weather."

"You'd better be careful," Walker warned. "There was a moose sighting in the woods before the ice storm. A bull, too, in broad daylight. Unusual for this time of year."

Overhearing him, Patience whined, "There's a moose in our woods?"

Even though Fern had told the children there might have been a moose wandering in the swampy area across the street from their house, she'd tried to present the possibility in a way that indicated the moose would be scared of *them*, not that they should be scared of the moose.

Walker must have heard the fear in Patience's voice because he punned, "Well, if there is, he's probably a *Chrismoose*, so you'd better leave some *Grischtdaag kuche* out for him!"

Phillip cracked up and Patience giggled,

too, but Fern anticipated the damage had been done; before Patience's bedtime, Fern was going to have to field a lot of questions about moose. *At least it will be better than answering any more questions about Walker picking me up in his buggy,* she thought.

When they arrived at the school, it was still in session, so Phillip and Patience hopped out of the carriage and ran to wait on the staircase for Jane.

"Sorry about that," Walker said to Fern, giving her a sheepish look. "I shouldn't have mentioned the moose in front of Patience."

"It's okay." Fern wanted to apologize for what she'd said about him picking her up at the library, but she would have felt awkward alluding to their courtship again.

Setting his gaze on the schoolhouse door, Walker nonchalantly asked, "What did Patience mean about going to the ice cream shop in the summer? Have you reconsidered selling the *haus*?"

"What? *Neh!*" Fern exclaimed.

Walker leaned back in the seat and Fern couldn't read his expression by his profile. Was he relieved? Disappointed? "Are you sure? Because if you did change your mind, that's fine with me."

"Fine with you?" she repeated dumbly.

"*Jah.* I mean, even though we told Anthony we were going to sell it, it's not too late to make other arrangements. The Lord has, ah, blessed me monetarily, so it's not as if I'm counting on the sale..."

Oh, so that was it. Walker was only letting her know if she changed her mind, it wouldn't put him under any financial duress. While she appreciated his assurance, Fern felt her heart settle an inch lower in her chest. *What was I expecting him to say? That he wants me to stay in Serenity Ridge?* She wouldn't, of course, even if he'd asked her to, so it was ridiculous to feel disappointed he hadn't. *It must be that seeing so many old sights has made me nostalgic*, she realized. *But I'm nos-*

talgic about being young, not about being with Walker.

"*Denki*, but staying here is Patience's prayer, not mine. I let her talk about the possibility because I don't want to discourage her from taking her requests to the Lord, but I absolutely intend to go through with the sale as soon as possible."

"I see," Walker replied noncommittally, just as someone flung open the school door so forcefully the wreath nearly flew off its hook. It was Jane.

She clamored down the stairs and exuberantly embraced each of her cousins. Then Phillip charged back to the buggy, but Patience unbuttoned her coat and Fern recognized she was showing Jane that she was wearing her old dress. Whatever Jane said in response caused Patience to hug her cousin a second time. As the girls joined hands and galloped across the schoolyard together, they reminded Fern so much of how close she'd once been to Gloria she didn't know whether to laugh or cry.

***

For the rest of their trip, Walker and Fern quietly listened to the children chattering about the evening's upcoming event. As Phillip's, Patience's and Jane's laughter filled the carriage, Walker found himself wishing Fern weren't so adamant about leaving Maine right away. Jane would have loved to have her cousins living so close by for a while longer, and they obviously would have enjoyed more time with her, too. *I wouldn't mind having Fern nearby, either. Now that we've broken the ice, I wonder why she's still in such a rush to leave.*

Ordinarily, Walker would have speculated Fern wanted to get back to Ohio because she had a suitor waiting for her there, but his mother informed him she'd found out on Sunday that Fern wasn't being courted. *I suppose it's none of my business why she's in a hurry to go,* he thought. *They're leaving soon and that's that. For tonight, it's a blessing for the* kinner *to be together.*

When they arrived at Walker's house, the children ran off to retrieve Jane's scooter from the barn. Fern and Walker went inside, where they found Walker's mother in a tizzy. She told them that afternoon Jaala had taken her to the phone shanty to call Willa, as was their Wednesday afternoon practice. But it was Willa's husband, Mark, who answered the phone at the agreed upon time. Apparently Willa and her children were suffering from high fevers and body aches. Willa could scarcely take care of herself, much less tend to her four little ones.

"Mark's beside himself. I regret missing Jane's program, but I ought to leave as soon as possible to help him. Since today was Jane's last day of school this week, I could take her with me, but I don't want her to come down with whatever Willa's *familye* has."

"Don't worry about Jane. She can

kumme to the tree farm with me in the mornings and then I'll take her to Roman's *haus* in the afternoons."

"Or you could drop her off at our *haus* before you go to work on Thursday and Friday," Fern immediately offered. "The *kinner* would be thrilled they get to spend two entire days together."

Walker didn't hesitate to accept. Although Jane could have played with the Swarey children at the farm, he knew she'd prefer to be with her cousins while she could. "I'll go call a driver," he said. There were two dependable *Englisch* drivers in Serenity Ridge and three more in Unity, so he was confident he'd be able to arrange transportation to the neighboring town.

"Louisa, you go pack. I'll put supper on the table," Fern suggested, and Walker's mother readily complied. They'd all finished their meal just as the driver pulled up shortly before six o'clock.

"It's too bad you're going to miss the

Grischtdaag program, *Groossmammi*," Jane expressed sincerely.

"I would have loved to see it, but I'm glad you recited your verses and sang the songs so often with me. I'll be able to picture it in my mind," Louisa replied. She bent to whisper something in her granddaughter's ear and Jane nodded in agreement.

Then Louisa gave everyone else a hug and wished Fern and her children a merry Christmas. As Walker escorted her to the van, she instructed him to call her at eleven a.m. on Saturday to make sure everyone had recovered enough for him and Jane to visit for Christmas.

"I will, *Mamm*—unless there's a blizzard and I can't make it to the phone shanty," Walker teased, but his mother was too worried for jokes.

"*Gott* willing, that won't happen, too," she murmured, wringing her hands. "But if it does, don't even think about venturing out into the snow. It's more important you and Jane stay safe than you arrive at Willa's for *Grischtdaag*."

After helping her into the van, Walker stood on the side porch, waving until the vehicle rolled out of sight. As he turned to open the door to the mudroom, he glanced through the kitchen window. Inside, Fern was washing the dishes and the children were drying and putting them away. Listening closely, he recognized they were singing, "All is calm, all is bright," which was exactly how he would have described the feeling in his heart at that moment.

Chapter Seven

Once they arrived at the schoolyard, the children rushed off so Jane could introduce Patience and Phillip to her friends before the program started, but Fern waited for Walker to hitch the horse. Standing just beyond the foot of the buggy, she balanced her container of peanut brittle atop two containers of sugar cookies Louisa had prepared. There was just enough moonlight to see the faces of other parents and children, and whether she recognized them from when she lived there or not, Fern exchanged warm greetings as they passed on their way into the building.

One man said hello and then stopped short and swung around. "Fern Troyer?" he asked incredulously.

"Jah," she said, answering to her maiden name.

He pulled his scarf away from his chin. "It's me, Stephen Hertig."

"Hello, Stephen, how are you?" Fern stalled. He obviously knew her when she lived in Serenity Ridge, but she hadn't seen him in church on Sunday and she couldn't immediately place him in her memory. Stephen must have noticed her hesitance because he chuckled.

"You've forgotten the first man to court you when you moved to Serenity Ridge?"

Fern instantly remembered—Stephen had only taken Fern out twice but that was enough for her to know he was charming, but he came on too strong for her taste. Judging from how openly he'd referred to their courtship just now, he was still as audacious as ever.

"My apologies. I didn't recognize you

with a beard. Is your wife inside? I'd like to meet her," she said emphatically, hoping to embarrass him into demonstrating more discretion.

"*Neh.*" Stephen tugged the brim of his hat lower. "She died last year from cancer."

"Oh, I'm so sorry!" Fern felt horrible. She softened her voice to confide, "My husband died from cancer, too."

She shifted the goodies to one arm so she could reach out and give his hand a sympathetic squeeze, but the containers slid across one another. Stephen grabbed the top two before they fell and Fern managed to keep her grasp on the bottom one.

"I can carry these in for you," he offered. "So, are you visiting or have you moved back to Serenity Ridge for *gut*?"

"*Neh.* I'm only here until *Samschdaag.* I, um, had some family business to take care of after my *onkel* Roman passed away."

"I was sorry to hear about that, although sometimes *Gott* works in mysterious ways. You never know what else He might have in mind by bringing you back to Serenity Ridge." It was too dark to be certain, but Fern thought he winked at her.

Unsettled, she simply thanked Stephen for his condolences. *What's taking Walker so long?* she wondered, just as she saw movement in her peripheral vision. Walker took a step forward and Fern noticed his hands were clenched.

"Hello, Stephen," he said curtly.

"Hi, Walker," Stephen replied with a grin. "Don't tell me you're the man responsible for keeping Fern waiting out here in the cold with her arms full?"

Walker's voice was so low it sounded like a growl. "Fern came with me because her *kinner* are Jane's *gschwischderkinner* and Jane invited them to see the *Grischtdaag* program. We ought to get inside now."

As Walker brusquely squeezed past Stephen and Fern and strode toward the school, Fern thought, *He sure made a point of letting Stephen know I'm only here with him because Jane wants Phillip and Patience to see the program.* Fern supposed his caution was understandable, considering how quickly rumors caught fire in their community. Still, she was flustered by Walker's gruffness.

Trying to make up for it, she conversationally asked Stephen, "How many *kinner* do you have?"

"None. Anke and I were only married for a year when she got sick, but *Gott* willing, I'll be blessed with lots of *seh* and *dochdere* when I remarry."

"Oh, you're remarrying?" Fern felt foolish for worrying Stephen had been flirting with her. "Is she someone from Serenity Ridge?"

"*Neh*, I was speaking hypothetically," Stephen said. "Right now, I'm on my own. I actually live in Unity—that's where Anke was from so we built a *haus* there. But I visit my *bruder*'s *familye* as often as I can. In fact, I came early for *Grischtdaag* to surprise my nieces and nephews. They have no idea I'll be here at the program tonight."

As they climbed the stairs to the school-house, Walker said over his shoulder, "It's almost time for the program to start. I've got to go talk to Abram for a minute. Fern, you'd better round up Phillip and Patience."

"I will, as soon as I deliver the goodies to the dessert table," Fern replied indig-nantly. *It would be nice if you gave me a hand instead of giving me instructions.*

"I'll help," Stephen offered, holding the door for her.

After Fern and Stephen eased their way through the crowd to add Fern's and Lou-isa's treats to the refreshment tables set up in the corner of the room, Stephen left to stand by his brother along the back wall with the rest of the men. The scholars, as the students were called, and the teacher had arranged two rows of chairs for the women; the teenagers and visiting children were expected to sit on the floor in front of them.

Fern spotted Phillip and Patience seated midway down the aisle with Jaala's grandchildren, but all the chairs behind them were filled. Fern waved and placed a finger to her lips to indicate they were to be quiet during the presentation, even though she had no doubt they'd be on their best behavior. Then she took a seat at the end of the row next to Eleanor Sutter, a young woman Fern knew when she lived in Maine. They had chatted briefly in church the previous Sunday, but this evening they barely had time to exchange greetings before the teacher walked to the front of the room and welcomed everyone to the event.

The first part of the program included a Biblical skit about the nativity story, Scriptural recitation, and songs by the scholars. Although there were no costumes or props, Fern noticed Phillip and Patience hung on every word, and she caught herself moving her own lips when Jane recited her verses. The young girl spoke distinctly and solemnly, without missing a word, and after she finished, Fern wicked away a tear. *Gloria would have been so delighted.* She scanned the back wall to see if Walker was standing nearby so she could give him a smile in acknowledgment of Jane's accomplishment, but he wasn't in her range of vision.

After the presentation, the school board awarded the teacher a financial gift, and then the audience was invited to sing Christmas hymns with the scholars. After the last song, the teacher announced the children would give the parents the gifts they'd made for them—a pencil case for their fathers and travel sewing kits for their mothers—and invited everyone to indulge in the refreshments.

As the women rose to their feet, Eleanor turned to Fern and remarked, "That was a *wunderbaar* program, wasn't it?"

"*Jah.* It was delightful. The children and

their teacher must have worked very hard on it." Fern craned her neck; she'd lost sight of Phillip and Patience.

"I couldn't help but notice you came in with Stephen Hertig," Eleanor hinted.

"*Jah.* He spotted me in the schoolyard and my arms were full so he helped me carry my desserts inside," Fern replied flatly. Eleanor had always been something of a gossip and Fern didn't want her to start any rumors. For that same reason, she didn't add that she'd actually come in with Walker, not Stephen.

Eleanor tittered. "There's no need to be coy with me, Fern. I understand if you want to keep it quiet that the two of you are striking up a long-distance courtship. I won't tell anyone."

Flabbergasted, Fern repeated, "Stephen was merely helping me car—"

But Eleanor spoke over her, saying, "Walker Huyard, my suitor, is very secretive about our relationship, too. He was so afraid of anyone finding out about it that on *Sunndaag* after we went out, he dropped me off at the end of my road instead of bringing me all the way home. Can you imagine?"

The din in the room was nothing compared to the racket inside Fern's head. *Walker is courting* Eleanor? Louisa had never mentioned Walker was courting anyone—and there was precious little the older woman hadn't told Fern about her children and grandchildren in the past few days. Fern couldn't exactly account for why she felt so let down to learn Walker was Eleanor's suitor, other than she couldn't imagine him choosing a woman like Eleanor. Then again, Fern never foresaw Walker marrying Gloria, either.

"Some people are more discreet than others," she replied pointedly.

"I suppose. But I hope when he gives me a ride home tonight, he doesn't expect me to walk down the lane in the cold and dark."

"Walker's giving you a ride home tonight?" Fern echoed. *He must have forgotten all about it.* Between the tumult of Phillip's tree-climbing escapade and Louisa's sudden departure, she could understand why it slipped his mind.

"*Jah.* Why do you sound so surprised?"

"Be-because I would have thought he'd have to get home early to put Jane to bed." She deliberately didn't tell Eleanor that Louisa had gone out of town. Nor did Fern say Walker was supposed to give her and the children a ride home, too; it was up to him, not her, to deliver that news to Eleanor.

"He's probably arranged for Jane and his *mamm* to ride home with someone else," Eleanor said, waving her hand. "It wouldn't be much *schpass* to have them tagging along."

It's not going to be any schpass *for me, either*, Fern silently lamented. *Especially if you're peeved at Walker for forgetting he'd made plans with you.*

Just then, Jane squeezed through the

cluster of people standing to Fern's left and announced, "This is for you!" She extended a box wrapped in gold paper and tied with a red bow.

Knowing the traveling sewing kits were intended for the scholars' mothers, Fern cooed, "Oh, Jane, that's so sweet! I would love to accept this, but don't you think your *groossmammi* might feel bad if you give it to me instead of her?"

"*Neh*. She told me I could," Jane insisted. "When you visit again you can bring it with you to hem the next dresses I hand down to Patience."

Moved by Jane's earnestness, as well as by her wish to have them visit again, Fern couldn't refuse. She thanked the girl, hugging her tightly and adding, "You did *wunderbaar* tonight. I could hear every word of your Bible verses, and I liked it that you smiled when you sang. I think the Lord must be very pleased with you."

"You do? Menno Ausberger said my

singing sounded like I have a cold, but I don't."

"Hmm. Maybe *he* has a cold and his ears are stuffed up," Fern suggested. "Anyway, you were singing for the Lord's ears, not Menno's."

"Hi, Jane!" Phillip had burst through the crowd with Patience in tow, and both of them immediately told Jane how much they liked the program. Since Eleanor was engaged in a conversation with someone else, Fern and the children slipped away to the dessert table, where they helped themselves to cookies and other treats. Patience wanted to see where Jane's desk was, so Fern settled the children around it to eat their snacks. But then Phillip spilled his cider and Fern went to fetch a napkin.

On the way back, she crossed paths with Stephen again. "I should have mentioned this earlier, but if you need anything while you're in town, I'll be right down the road at my *bruder*'s *haus*," he said.

Fern bit her bottom lip, wavering about

whether to ask him for a lift home. After the kind of remarks Stephen made earlier, she didn't want him to get any ideas about her being interested in him romantically, but it would be awkward for all three adults if Fern "tagged along" with Eleanor and Walker. Reluctantly, she answered, "If, um, if you wouldn't mind giving the *kinner* and me a ride home tonight, I'd appreciate it."

Stephen's eyes lit up. "Of course I don't mind! I was on my way to hitch my horse now."

Circling back to tell Phillip and Patience it was time to go, Fern discovered the cider had been mopped up and Walker was leaning against the wall by the window near where they were eating. "Oh, there you are!" she exclaimed. "Listen, the *kinner* and I are going to leave now. I've arranged for someone else to take us home—"

"Why would you do that?" Walker interrupted.

Fern hadn't planned to tell him about her conversation with Eleanor. Considering how hard he'd worked to keep his courtship a secret, Fern figured it would embarrass Walker that she knew about it. Instead, she'd intended to say it would be less strain on Walker's horse if Stephen gave her a ride, since he lived much closer to Roman's house. But she was so ruffled by Walker's accusatory tone, she snitched, "Because *you* apparently forgot you were giving Eleanor a ride home. It's one thing if you have your *dochder* with you, but I don't think she'll appreciate three more people in the buggy."

"What are you talking about?" Walker cupped Fern's elbow and steered her farther away from the children. "I'm not giving Eleanor a ride home. Why would you think I was?"

"Because she told me you were."

He shook his head. "*Neh.* That's not the truth."

Fern bristled. "Are you saying *I'm* not

telling the truth about Eleanor telling *me* that or *Eleanor's* not telling the truth about *you* telling *her* that?"

"I'm saying I never had any plans to give Eleanor a ride home, so someone is mistaken." Walker crossed his arms. "And it isn't me."

"Well, my ears work fine, so I'm not the one who's mistaken, either," Fern retorted. "I guess that means Eleanor must have dreamed it all up! Just like she must have imagined you're her suitor and you went out with her on *Sunndaag.*"

The complacence melted from Walker's face. He faltered backward, dropping his arms to his sides. "I—I—I *did* go for a walk with her, but I never said I'd take her home. And I'm certainly not courting her—or anyone else, for that matter. She must have gotten the wrong impression."

Just like I *must have gotten the wrong impression about how you felt about* me? Fern took a deep breath and let it out before responding. "Apparently, there's been a misunderstanding, and I wish you two the best in working it out, but I have to go. Stephen is waiting—"

"*Stephen* is bringing you home?" Walker sneered. "Then by all means, you ought to hurry off to be with him. Don't give us a second thought!"

Fern had had enough. "What is your problem?"

"We had an agreement! It isn't right for you to change your mind after making plans with me."

It's only a buggy ride—you *changed* your *mind about committing to spend the rest of your life with me!* Fern's cheeks prickled with heat. Digging her fingernails into her hand, she stared Walker down and replied as evenly as she could, "For one thing, I thought I was doing you a favor, so you wouldn't get into hot water with Eleanor. For another, I don't see what the big deal is about Stephen bringing me home."

* * *

"The big deal," Walker articulated deliberately, "is that Jane was looking forward to taking Patience and Phillip past a specially decorated *haus* in an *Englisch* neighborhood. It was supposed to be a surprise."

Fern blinked, but she kept her chin in the air. "Well, I'm sorry about that, but as I said, I was trying to help you out of a sticky situation. Good night, Walker."

She swished over to the children, who were now flipping through a book, and crouched down next to Jane. Walker couldn't hear what Fern said, but he could tell by their expressions that all three children were crushed their evening together was ending prematurely. As Walker moved closer, Fern consoled them, "You'll get to see each other tomorrow."

After Fern and her children departed, Walker told Jane to say goodbye to her teacher, get her coat and meet him by the door. Meanwhile, he needed to find Eleanor before she spread more rumors about the two of them. Instead, Eleanor spotted him first, tapping his shoulder from behind. "Is it time for us to go yet?" she whispered into his ear. "Just tell me where you want me to meet you."

He twirled around. "Why did you tell Fern we're courting?"

Eleanor's eyes widened. "She told you I told her? That makes her an even bigger *boubelmoul* than what people accuse me of being! I guess that means I don't have to keep quiet about her and Stephen Hertig, either. Did you know they've reunited?"

Walker already sensed there might have been some interest between Stephen and Fern from the way they were cozying up to each other outside the schoolhouse. Not to mention, she was clearly eager to ride home with him.

"What Fern and Stephen do is none of our business," Walker reminded Eleanor—and himself. "What I want to know is why you told her *we're* courting."

Eleanor peeked at him from beneath her eyelashes. "I'm sorry. I know how private you are and I shouldn't have mentioned it. But sometimes, *gut* news is worth sharing."

"What are you talking about? We aren't courting. I never said I'd give you a ride home, either!"

"If you didn't want to be my suitor, why did you ask to spend time alone with me?" Eleanor squished her mouth into a pout.

Walker stammered, "I—I—I asked your *bruder* to *kumme* hiking with us, too. I wanted to enjoy hiking in the pleasant weather with friends, that's all."

"Then why did you agree to take me home tonight?"

Walker was adamant. "I *didn't*."

"*Jah*, you did. I remember the exact spot on the trail. I told you about helping my nephew memorize his Bible verses and then I said it would be romantic if you and

I could go for a ride after the program and look at all the *Englischers*' homes decorated with lights. And you agreed."

"Did I?" The details of what Eleanor was describing were hazy, but Walker vaguely remembered her talking about the Christmas program. He'd been so preoccupied Sunday afternoon, it was entirely possible he'd mumbled agreement to almost anything she'd said. "I'm sorry. I don't remember saying that."

"Well, you *did*. And I've already told my *familye* I'd get a ride with one of my friends, so they left without me."

Walker swallowed. "I can take you home, then." Wanting to emphasize that this didn't mean he'd changed his mind about courting her, he added, "As your neighbor, I mean, not as someone who wants to be your suitor."

"Walker Huyard, I wouldn't accept a ride from you if it was forty degrees below and I had to walk home barefoot, much less allow you to be my suitor!" Eleanor ranted. "I don't know what Gloria saw in you, but it certainly wasn't charm or *gut* manners."

Walker didn't defend himself. Regardless of whether Eleanor had misinterpreted his intentions, he was partly to blame. He never should have asked her out for a walk in order to avoid spending time with Fern, and he deserved every irate word Eleanor hurled at him. "I really am sorry," was all he could say before she stomped off.

In the buggy, Jane was uncharacteristically sullen; Walker blamed Fern for souring what should have been a special celebration. When they got home, she went straight to bed, but Walker stayed up, fuming. *Eleanor may have had a reason to be angry at me, but Fern didn't. She ruined my* dochder's *surprise, yet she acted as if she was doing me a favor!*

For the next hour, Walker couldn't stop thinking about Fern riding home with Stephen Hertig and what Eleanor had said about the two of them. Walker was aware

Stephen had once courted Fern, but she'd said he wasn't her type. However, it appeared she may have changed her mind. *Fern's emotions are as capricious as ever*, he carped to himself. *I wouldn't be surprised if she changes her mind about selling the* haus, *too, now that she's rekindled her flame with Stephen.*

Walker's ornery thoughts plagued him long into the night, and the next morning he rose with a whopper of a headache. He retrieved two aspirin from the medicine cabinet and shuffled into the kitchen for a glass of water. Jane was already at the table, glumly pushing her cereal around in the bowl.

"Do you have a *bauchweh*?" he asked, figuring her tummy hurt from all the treats she'd eaten the evening before.

"Neh," she said, dragging her fingers across her eyes. "I'm sad."

Walker's chest tightened with renewed anger at Fern. Trying to temper it, he took a swallow of water before asking, "Because you didn't get to show Patience and Phillip the *haus* last night?"

"*Neh.*" Jane could hardly utter the word.

"Then what is it, Jane?"

"You didn't say anything about the pencil case I made for you," she burst out. "Don't you like it?"

Walker smacked his forehead. He'd been so consumed with Fern for being thoughtless and hurting his daughter's feelings he'd forgotten all about the gift. "Ach! Jane—I'm sorry. I tucked it into my coat for safekeeping and I never even opened it. Let me take a look now."

Never one to hold a grudge, Jane leaped from her chair and bounded toward the mudroom. "I'll get it!"

After Walker carefully unwrapped his present, he examined it carefully, complimenting Jane's handiwork as he slid the top open and shut and turned the case over to admire how she'd carved his initials on the bottom.

"I've never had such a handy pencil

case. I'll treasure it always," he said, kissing her cheek. "Now, we'd better eat our breakfast or I'll be late for work."

On the way to Roman's house, Jane asked, "Since we didn't get to show everybody the *Englisch haus* last night, can we go tonight, *Daed*?"

"Oh, I don't think that will work out." Given the tension between him and Fern, he was dreading even seeing her briefly this morning. "I'll probably finish working in the yard by four o'clock and the *Englischers'* lights don't *kumme* on until six o'clock."

"We could stay at *Groossdaadi*'s *haus* and eat supper with them until it's time for the lights to *kumme* on," Jane proposed.

"It's not polite to invite ourselves to supper. Fern might not have enough food for us."

Jane had a solution for that, too. "You could let her take our buggy to the grocery store while you're working in the yard with Phillip. Patience and I can help her make supper."

"Jane, I said *neh*."

She paused before timidly questioning, "*Daed*, are you mad Fern and Patience and Phillip rode home with Micah's *onkel* instead of us?"

Walker was shocked his daughter had picked up on his feelings. Was he that transparent? He chose his words carefully. "I was disappointed because I knew how much you wanted to show Phillip and Patience the lights. I didn't want you to be upset."

"I *was* a little upset," Jane confessed. "But now I'm not. My teacher says sometimes people hurt our feelings even when they have *gut* tensions."

"*Gut* tensions?"

"*Jah*. It means they want to do something *gut*, but they end up doing something bad. Like when I made tea to surprise *Groossmammi* and I broke her favorite teacup. Remember?"

"Jah." Walker marveled at his daughter's comprehension.

"My teacher says we shouldn't be quick to judge because we can't see what's in someone's heart. Only *Gott* can do that. But Fern told me she didn't want to wear out Daisy's legs, and Micah's *haus* is closer to *Groossdaadi*'s *haus* than ours is. So I think her heart has *gut* tensions in it."

Walker was stunned silent. His daughter had just unwittingly described what had happened between him and Fern eight years ago: his intentions in marrying Gloria had been good, but he'd caused Fern incredible pain. In light of that, Walker realized how hypocritical it was for him to harbor resentment toward her over something as minor as changing their transportation arrangements, especially since she did it to help him out.

"Your teacher is very wise," he said. "I'm *hallich* you're taking her lessons to heart."

Proving she was still a child despite her momentary insightfulness, Jane wheedled, "Could we invite Fern and Patience and Phillip to go out for pizza at Mario's? We could take them to see the lights after we eat. Please, *Daed*?"

"*Jah*, okay, if they want to go," he relented. *And if their* mamm *forgives me for behaving like a* dummkopf.

So when Fern came to the door, Walker asked if he could speak with her in private. She welcomed Jane into the house and stepped onto the porch, tugging the door shut behind her. Folding her arms across her chest, she raised an eyebrow at him. "Whatever you have to say, please make it quick. I'm cold."

Walker cleared his throat. "I, uh, wanted to apologize for how I spoke to you last night. I was disappointed Jane's plans were ruined and I was upset about the situation with Eleanor. But I shouldn't have spoken so rudely to you, especially since you were trying to spare me from conflict with Eleanor." He chuckled self-deprecatingly. "Not that it helped—she was awfully mad at me."

"It's nothing to be *glib* about. You hurt her feelings. She thought you cared about her. She probably thought she had a future with you." Fern shook her head and looked away. Were those tears glinting in her eyes?

"I wasn't being glib. I felt *baremlich* about the miscommunication," Walker contended. "But Eleanor *shouldn't* have assumed we had a future together. I never told her I wanted one."

"What was she supposed to think? You took her out alone on *Sunndaag*."

Walker held up his hands. "I invited her to go hiking, *jah*, but I invited her *bruder* to *kumme*, too. But I wouldn't have even asked him if I weren't so desperate to get out of the *haus* when—" Walker closed his mouth but it was too late.

"When I was visiting your *mamm*?" Fern huffed.

He rubbed his gloved hand over his eyes. "It—it seemed as if you didn't want me around..." Walker's cheeks were scorched with humiliation.

Fern sighed. "You're right. I wasn't very *freindlich* to you at the attorney's office. I was...overwhelmed that morning."

Walker knew there was more to their reasons for avoiding each other on Sunday than that, but he let it go. Daring to look at her again, he asked, "Will you please forgive me for how I acted last night?"

"*Jah*, if you'll forgive me for being so standoffish at Anthony's office and in *kurrich* on *Sunndaag*," she agreed. "And I *am* sorry I spoiled Jane's surprise."

Grinning, Walker said, "As it happens, I talked to her about it and we wondered if you'd want to go see the *Englischers'* lights tonight. They don't turn them on until six, but I'd like to treat you all to supper at Mario's pizzeria first." *Unless you made plans with Stephen already?*

Walker held his breath until a smile widened Fern's rosy cheeks and she replied, "*Denki.* That would be *wunderbaar.*"

A few minutes later, as Walker's horse clip-clopped along the road to the Christmas tree farm, he reflected on his conversation with Fern. Although he was relieved she'd forgiven him for behaving like a dolt the evening before, he caught himself wishing he could tell her why he'd married Gloria. There had been plenty of other times over the years when Walker longed to confide in her, but he'd never felt as tempted as he did right now.

It wasn't just that he wanted to absolve himself in her eyes—although that definitely would have been part of his motivation. It was also that he wanted to release Fern from the pain he recognized she still carried. He'd just seen it in her eyes and heard it in her voice when she'd rebuked Walker for hurting Eleanor's feelings. *It was as if she'd been talking about what happened with me and her, not with me and Eleanor.*

But Walker had made a promise, for Jane's sake, and no matter how much he wanted to ease Fern's burden, he couldn't give in to the desire to tell her why he'd really married Gloria. *In a couple of days, she'll be gone and the feeling will pass*, he told himself.

The startling thing was, he didn't know if he wanted it to.

Chapter Eight

After Walker left, Fern went upstairs to where the children were playing a card game Jane had brought with her. When she asked Jane if she could speak to her alone, the three of them exchanged furtive glances, but the young girl followed Fern back down to the living room. Fern sat on the sofa and Jane stood a few feet in front of her with her head tipped downward, as if she was concerned she was about to receive a scolding.

"Your *daed* told me about the surprise you had planned for last night. I'm sorry we didn't get to see the lights, but he asked me if we could go see them tonight and I said *jah*." Fern thought this would bring a smile to Jane's chubby face, but the girl furrowed her forehead.

"Didn't he ask you to *kumme* to Mario's with us, too?"

"Oh, *jah*! I think that's a *wunderbaar* idea."

Jane beamed, exposing something brown stuck to her teeth. "*I* thought of it."

Fern experienced a flash of disappointment that the idea had come from Jane instead of from Walker. *That's* lappich, she told herself. *It's not as if it's a date...* Rather than reminding Jane it was prideful to boast, Fern said, "I'm glad you did. Now, do you want to tell Phillip and Patience about it or do you still want to keep it a secret until we get there?"

"Oh, I'd better tell them. It's too hard to keep a secret for even one day and I already kept this for one-and-a-half days."

Chuckling, Fern agreed, "You're right about that. But before you go tell Phillip and Patience our plans, how about if I brush your hair for you?" Fern didn't want to hurt Jane's feelings, but she noticed her hair was coming out of its bun and she suspected Walker had forgotten to help her with it. She also figured he'd forgotten to remind her to brush her teeth.

"Okay. I usually brush the snarls out and then *Groossmammi* helps me pin it, but today I did it by myself and it feels all slippery," Jane said, clearly not at all embarrassed by Fern's offer.

Fern went to get a brush. When she returned, the young girl had released her hair from its elastic, and it flowed down past her shoulders in subtle waves. She stood with her back to Fern, who told her, "Your *mamm* had a pretty natural wave to her hair like you do, you know that?"

"Really?"

"*Jah.* Didn't your *daed* ever tell you that?"

"*Neh.* But he told me she had brown hair."

Brown? Gloria's hair was caramel-colored and accented with strands of honey from the summer sun. *Walker told me my eyes were the color of stars, yet he couldn't describe Gloria's beautiful hair other than to say it was brown?* Trying to convince herself she wasn't being nosy, she only wanted to find out so she could add to Jane's knowledge about Gloria, Fern asked, "What else did your *daed* say about your *mamm*?"

Jane shrugged. "He said *mamm* didn't need to have any more *bobblin* because she loved me so much that one *bobble* was enough. That's why I don't have any *breider* or *schwesdere*."

And because Gloria passed away before she could have more kinner, Fern thought sadly. She pinned Jane's prayer *kapp* on over her tidy bun and then drew the child backward for a hug. "That's true, she did love you very, very much."

"You knew me when I was little?" Jane asked, snuggling closer, just like Patience always did.

"*Neh*, but your *mamm* often talked to me about how much she wanted to have a *dochder* one day." Actually, Gloria used to claim she wanted four daughters and four sons. Fern sniffed away a tear and when she did, she caught a whiff of chocolate. She turned Jane to face her and asked, "Did you have candy for breakfast?"

Jane clasped her hands over her mouth, her voice muffled as she explained, "It's from my teacher. All the scholars get a box of special candy after the *Grischtdaag* program."

"And you were eating it upstairs with Phillip and Patience?"

Jane ducked her head. "*Jah.*"

Fern lifted Jane's chin with a finger so she had to look into Fern's eyes. "Do you know the one thing that's even harder to keep to yourself for two days than a secret?" she asked and Jane shook her head. "A box of candy."

The young girl giggled, and now Fern could see it was chocolate dimming her teeth. She suggested Jane go rinse her mouth and then she accompanied her upstairs. Phillip and Patience wore guilty expressions as Jane bent to slide the box of candy from where they'd hidden it beneath the bed and handed it over to Fern. "I'll put it away for you so you don't get a *bauchweh*. You wouldn't want to be too sick to go you-know-where."

"Where?" Phillip and Patience asked at the same time. Jane barely had the answer out of her mouth before they sprang to their feet in excitement.

When they settled down, Fern instructed her children to brush their teeth again, and then she sent all three of them outside to burn off their chocolate-induced hyperactivity. She wished she had their energy; last night she'd stayed awake stewing over Walker's behavior until almost midnight. Yawning as she went about her morning chores, she reflected on his apology. They'd rarely argued while they were courting, but after they did, his entire body, face and voice would seem weighed down with contrition, just as it had today. Except this morning his frown was even more pronounced because his mustache dragged at the corners, too.

Thinking about Walker's mustache made Fern wonder why he hadn't remarried. When he was her suitor and they discussed their dreams about having a family, he always said he hoped the Lord blessed him with between four and six children. Given how pushy Louisa was, Fern imagined in the five years since Gloria died, Walker's mother must have tried to match him with one of the unmarried women in Serenity Ridge or Unity. Yet here he was, still unmarried and with only one child.

It occurred to Fern maybe Walker didn't want to marry again because he was so anguished over Gloria's death that he still hadn't recovered from the loss. Perhaps in his mind, no one would ever compare to her. Fern felt a jolt of envy at the possibility. She'd once longed to love and be loved like that. In fact, she'd once thought she *had* loved and been loved like that...

I shouldn't be entertaining thoughts that will only lead to resentment and I shouldn't be speculating about Walker's relationship with Gloria, either. Fern wrung the rag she'd been using under the faucet. *For now, I'm just glad that Walker and I aren't at odds with each other anymore.*

But if she was really so glad, why did she feel like weeping?

Usually Fridays and Saturdays were the busiest days on the Christmas tree farm, but on Thursday morning, the place was bustling with procrastinators and with those people whose tradition it was to wait until Christmas Eve to buy a tree. According to the owner, Levi Swarey, the *Englischers* were nervous about the storm that was forecast to potentially begin the next afternoon and continue into Saturday, so they'd swarmed the farm to get their trees while they could.

It was almost two o'clock by the time Walker left, and on the way to Roman's house, he hastily took a few bites of the sandwich he'd made. Patience, Phillip and Jane were perched on the fence bordering Roman's front yard when Walker arrived. He waved and they raced through the yard to beat him to the barn.

"Fern said *jah*!" Jane announced as soon as he stepped out of the carriage, even though Walker already knew Fern agreed to go out that evening. "Guess how many hours there are until the *Englischers* turn on their lights, *Daed*."

"Eighteen?" Walker kidded her.

"*Neh*. There were only four hours the last time we asked Fern. It's even less now."

As Jane and her cousins took off to race up the hill, Walker thought, *Poor Fern. Jane's so excited she's probably been asking her what time it is every half hour.*

But Fern seemed unruffled when she beckoned him from the porch. "I was just going to put the kettle on for tea. You're *wilkom* to *kumme* in if you'd like to sit down for a few minutes."

Walker approached so he wouldn't have to shout. "*Denki*, but I'd better get to work right away. Supposedly the nor'easter they predicted last week might start tomorrow afternoon. Its path is still uncertain, but if it does hit, it should continue snowing right into *Samschdaag* morning. So I want to make as much progress as I can on the trees today."

Fern's expression was pinched. "Ach. I hope the snow doesn't interfere with our travel plans." She asked if they could stop at the phone shanty that evening so she could touch base with the van driver, and Walker agreed. Before going indoors again, she offered to call Phillip over to give a hand with the logs.

"Don't do that—let him play."

"I think he needs a separation from the *meed* and they need one from him, too."

"Really? They've been getting along so well."

"*Jah*. Even better than we have," Fern remarked, impishly tilting her chin up at him. "But if Phillip really is more of a help than a hindrance, I'd appreciate it if he could work with you as often as possible while we're still here. He's learning so much from you. He quotes nearly everything you say."

Walker's face warmed. "I enjoy being around him, too—and not just because he's closer to the ground than I am so he can pick up all the debris I'm too stiff to bend over and get." Then he asked, "Has Jane been pestering you all day about the time?"

"Only every ten minutes." Walker groaned but Fern just laughed. "I think it's *wunderbaar* she's so excited about sharing something special with her *gschwischderkinner*. Gloria was the same way—I remember how eager she was to take me to Serenity Lake for the first time. Or to Brubaker's. Not that Jane was old enough to have learned it from her, but it's amusing to see that the two of them are alike in that regard."

Walker tried hard to remember Gloria ever being enthusiastic in the same way Jane was, but he couldn't. After Jordan's death he'd been in such a fog, and once Jane was born, most of Walker's attention was focused on her, not on Gloria. Walker realized he probably hadn't noticed a lot of other qualities in his wife, either. While he strove to be the best father he could be to Jane, he realized he hadn't been much of a husband to Gloria. He'd thought he'd at least been a good friend, but in retrospect, he had his doubts. It couldn't have been easy for Gloria to live with him—not because he was mean, but because he was distant. He was *absent*. Thinking about it now made him wince.

"I'm sorry," Fern said. "I won't talk

about Gloria anymore if it makes you miss her too much."

"That's okay." Walker understood Fern's need to reminisce about her cousin, especially now that she was surrounded by memories of living with her in Serenity Ridge. "It—it's just there are things I can't recall very well about her."

Fern touched his arm. "Sometimes it seems like I can't recall the things I want to remember and I can only remember the things I want to forget," she empathized.

"*Jah*. That's exactly how it is with me, too," he admitted, locking his gaze with hers until Phillip came tearing around the house. Fern quickly dropped her hand and stepped backward. When the boy came stomping up the stairs and halted right between them, Walker said, "I hope you've *kumme* to help me."

"*Jah*. I need to work up my appetite again because you're taking us out to a restaurant for pizza. We hardly ever get to go to a restaurant."

"Phillip, we don't want to take advantage of Walker's generosity to us," Fern scolded him.

"It's okay. I only ate half my sandwich today so my *bauch* will have room for lots of pizza, too," Walker said. "C'mon, Phillip, it's your turn to get the wheelbarrow and tarp. I'll carry the ax and saws."

By the time it was dusk and Fern called Phillip in to wash up, Walker only had a small pile of logs to split. He figured it wouldn't take him more than ninety minutes to finish everything the next day, including replacing the shingles on the roof. After he'd put away their supplies and tools, Walker went inside to wash his hands and face before heading back out to hitch the buggy.

"At this pizza place, they give *kinner* a loopy straw and you can take it home," Jane informed her cousins on the way into town. "I have a red one, a green one and a blue one but not a yellow one."

"If I get a yellow one, we can trade," Patience offered.

Phillip surmised admiringly, "You must get to eat out a lot if you already have three loopy straws."

To the children's delight, there was a toy train running around a large Christmas tree in the corner of the restaurant. They went over to watch it while Fern and Walker placed their order and chose a table. Walker seated himself across from Fern. Her eyes shimmered and her voice warbled as she relayed the story of how she'd discovered the children had been eating chocolate in Patience's room that morning. Walker cracked up when she said she'd noticed how dingy Jane's teeth looked and she thought he'd forgotten to tell her to brush them.

"Actually," he confessed, "I *did* forget to tell her to brush them, but she's usually pretty consistent about doing that without a reminder. I forgot to tell her to brush her hair, too, but I can see you must have helped her out with that."

"It's so thick and wavy, it's no wonder she has a hard time pinning it," Fern replied as a customer holding a boxed pizza stopped at their table. Because he was wearing jeans and a flannel jacket instead of a suit and tie, it took a moment for Walker to recognize who the man was.

"Hi, Anthony," Walker and Fern both greeted him at the same time.

"Hello, Fern and Walker. What a nice surprise to see you together," he said. "I—I mean both at once. I was going to stop by Roman's house tomorrow but it might snow, so I'm glad I caught you here. Have you made any decisions about whether you want any of Roman's possessions?"

"We've been having so much fun, I actually forgot all about doing that," Fern exclaimed. "There might be a tool or two I'd like to take, and one of the quilts my *ant* made—I want the *kinner* to have something useful from their great *ant* and *onkel*. Otherwise, as I mentioned, I think we should give Roman's belongings away or sell them with the house." She added, "If Walker doesn't mind, that is."

Happy that Fern had enjoyed their time together, despite their squabble, he agreed with her. Anthony chatted with Walker about his progress on the trees and Walker assured him he'd have everything cleaned up by the next day. Since the following Monday was Christmas, Anthony said he'd wait until after the holiday to talk to his real estate contact.

"We might not be able to officially get the ball rolling until after the first of the year, but just as soon as I have more information, I'll let you both know," the attorney promised. "Unless you change your mind about leaving, Fern."

Walker scrutinized her face, trying to read her reaction. Fern smiled slightly before replying, "I don't think that's going to happen, but I'll let you know if it does."

*"I don't think that's going to happen"
isn't the same as saying she wants to stay,
but it's a far cry from a few days ago when
she said she had no intention of ever living in Maine again*, Walker noticed. *What
changed?* He wondered if it was because
she really *did* have hopes of developing
a relationship with Stephen. Then he noticed the children had approached the
table and were standing behind Anthony;
Fern probably didn't want to give the law-
yer a flat-out *no* in front of the three of
them, especially Patience.

"Okay, well, I wish you safe travels—
and don't hesitate to get in touch if there's
anything I can do." Anthony rapped his
knuckle on the table twice and turned to
leave, almost stumbling over the children
on his way.

A moment after he left, the server arrived with their pizza and drinks. As soon
as everyone lifted their heads after saying grace, Jane pointed out, "Look, I got

a purple loopy straw. That's even better than a yellow one!"

Since they were all ravenous, they ate in relative silence. Phillip and Walker polished off a pepperoni and sausage pizza between them, while Fern and the girls shared the other, since they preferred to only have cheese on theirs.

When the server brought Walker the check, she commented to Fern, "If you don't mind me saying, you have such a nice family. I wish my children were as well behaved as the three of yours."

"Did you hear that?" Patience remarked to Jane once the woman went back behind the counter. "She thinks we're *schweschdere.*"

"That's probably because you're wearing one of my dresses."

Smiling ear to ear, Patience added, "And because we look a lot alike."

Walker had to bite down on his tongue to keep from laughing out loud; the two girls were as different as night and day. *As different as Gloria and Fern.*

"That lady must think *Mamm* is married to you, Walker," Phillip deducted. "She doesn't know you aren't any relation to us."

Logically, Walker understood the boy was only repeating what he'd had impressed upon him by Fern—which was partly why it was so painful to hear— but he felt as if he'd been whacked in the chest with a sledgehammer. Reeling, he couldn't reply.

Fern noticed the shadow that crossed Walker's face and the way his posture went slack. Trying to compensate for Phillip's remark—a remark *she* never should have stated so adamantly to him in the first place—Fern said, "*Denki* for the *appenditlich* supper, Walker. It was a real treat and we enjoyed it. Didn't we, Patience and Phillip?"

Phillip stopped slurping the last of his

milk with his straw to raise his head. "*Jah,* it was the best pizza I ever ate. And the most. *Denki.*"

Fern glanced at Patience to prompt her to thank Walker, too. Astonishingly, the girl bounced up from her chair, scuffed around the table to where Walker was sitting and threw her arms around his neck. "*Denki,* Walker." Before letting go, she whispered something into his ear that returned the sparkle to his eyes.

My dear, sweet, sensitive dochder, Fern thought as she crossed the room to the coatrack. She reached for her coat, but it snagged on the hook and she nearly pulled the entire rack forward on top of herself.

"Here, let me," Walker offered, reaching over her to steady the coatrack. He lifted hers and held it behind her so she could slide her arms through her sleeves. And tonight he held the door for her, too, just like he used to do when they were courting. It seemed like such a small thing, but

Fern missed having a man extend courtesies like these.

Despite the children's protests, they stopped at the phone shanty first, since it was on the way to the *Englischer*'s house. Using Walker's flashlight so she could see to dial, Fern called the van driver, who was scheduled to take her and the children to the bus station in Waterville. He indicated if the nor'easter hit, it would be a doozy, and he suggested Fern ought to consider leaving the next morning to beat the snow.

"Since it's not coming from the west, it won't affect states like New York and Ohio, so you'll be fine if you catch the morning bus tomorrow," he surmised. "But if you take a chance and wait until Saturday and it *does* snow as much as they say it might, you probably won't be able to dig out until late Sunday. Which means you won't make it out of Maine until Tuesday, since Monday is Christmas and the buses aren't running."

Fern dithered. She supposed she could call the station and change her travel date, but she'd given her word to Walker that she'd watch Jane tomorrow morning while he was at work. Of course, he'd understand why she needed to leave early, but the children would be terribly disappointed. Especially Patience, who was already dragging her feet. So Fern told the driver she wasn't prepared to leave until Saturday.

"Okay, but if you don't see me by five thirty a.m., it's because I'm snowed in," the driver cautioned. "Although I suppose if I'm snowed in, the bus will be snowed in, too, so it won't matter if I don't show up."

Next Fern called and left a voice-mail message at the phone shanty nearest Adam's house, indicating that she might be delayed by the snowstorm and she'd call if she was still on schedule to arrive in Ohio late Saturday evening. She figured calling them if she *was* returning on time would be much easier than calling if she *wasn't*.

"Is everything all set?" Walker asked her when she got back into the buggy.

"Jah," she said, not telling him she'd passed up the opportunity to leave a full day earlier. She didn't want him to feel guilty if she stayed in order to watch Jane, nor did she want him to try to convince her it was okay to go.

They saw the glow of the lights even before they rounded the corner to the lavishly decorated house. Walker pulled off to the side of the road so everyone could get out for a better look. Unlike many other *Englischers'* yards, this one contained no lawn ornaments or other types of decorations, except for lights. A rainbow of colors outlined the house and garage, wound around the fence, spiraled up the tree trunks and dripped from the branches. There must have been a hundred lights on the mailbox alone. The display was probably even considered garish by

Englisch standards, but something about it was mesmerizing.

"I don't know which is brighter—the lights or the expressions on the *kinners'* faces," Fern murmured as she watched Jane, Patience and Phillip taking in the spectacle.

"What did you say?" Walker leaned toward her. As she repeated it into his ear, she noticed the soft fullness of his beard, which looked more coppery than chestnut beneath the multicolor lights. She hadn't been this close to him since—

"Mamm!" Phillip pulled her hand. "Look at that star at the top of the pine tree!"

Walker straightened his posture and Fern did, too. "I see it," she said. "I wonder how they got it up there."

"Too bad they didn't ask Walker to do it. He's the best ladder climber I've ever seen."

"Neh, not me," Walker answered modestly, but Fern could tell he was touched

by Phillip's admiration. Sometimes her boy's bluntness made Fern cringe, but other times he would come out with a compliment that made a person grin from ear to ear, the way Walker was doing as he replied, "Whoever hung that star probably used a bucket truck to get up there."

"How could a person fit in a bucket?" Phillip wanted to know.

As Walker described the kind of truck he had referenced, Fern and the girls silently marveled at the lights. After a few more minutes, they all returned to the buggy. When they were seated again, Patience said with a sigh, "I wish this night would never end."

"If your *mamm* says it's okay, it doesn't have to end yet," Walker announced. "I've got a surprise up my sleeve."

"Is it up your shirtsleeve or your coat sleeve?" Phillip was seriously trying to figure out what kind of surprise he could have hidden in his clothing, and Fern hoped his question didn't seem insolent to Walker.

But Walker just patiently replied, "It's not up my *actual* sleeve. The surprise is a place." Once Fern agreed they could extend their outing a little longer, he commanded, "Everybody sit back in your seats, and no fair peeking, Jane. You either, Fern."

Fern promptly closed her eyes, and the children started guessing where Walker was taking them. Jane thought they were going to the bowling alley and Phillip guessed they were going ice skating. Patience supposed the library was their destination.

"I'll give you a hint. It's someplace we wouldn't normally go in the winter."

"I know—Serenity Lake!" Fern exclaimed, opening her eyes.

"Hey, I said no peeking!" Walker extended his arm straight out to shield her face, but she pushed his hand down. So he crooked his arm around her head from behind and covered her eyes with his gloved fingers, drawing her toward him. "You'll find out when we get there," he promised in a voice that was husky and low and made Fern's heart quiver.

She knew she ought to try to wriggle out of Walker's grasp—if the children peeked, they might have seen—but she couldn't make herself move a muscle. Did being so close make him feel as breathless as she felt? Did it make him want to stop time—or to turn it back to when they used to embrace for real, not as part of a guessing game?

"Okay, on the count of three, you can all open your eyes again," Walker directed everyone a few minutes later, releasing his hold on Fern.

"One, two—"

"Foster's Creamery!" Jane shouted.

"*Jah*. Should we go inside or do we want to take our orders to go?" Walker teased.

"Inside!" the children and Fern answered in unison.

Walker and Fern secured a small booth for the two of them, but the children perched atop the swivel stools at the counter. The girls ordered junior hot-fudge sundaes. Phillip wanted to imitate Walker and get a regular-sized banana split, but Fern would only let him order the smaller size because a swivel stool and a large banana split seemed like a precarious combination for his stomach. Fern ordered a single scoop of white chocolate and raspberry.

Having downed his banana split before Fern had eaten half of her cone, Walker studied her as she licked the white-and-pink dessert. Self-conscious, she shivered noticeably, which made her feel even more diffident. "Ice cream always makes me shiver—even in the summer."

"I remember."

He remembers? Fern shivered again and quickly finished the rest of her cone.

By the time Walker brought Fern, Patience and Phillip home, Patience was so tired she practically sleepwalked into the house and up the stairs.

"This was my favorite day," she murmured drowsily as Fern tucked her in. *"Gut nacht, Mamm."*

When she went into Phillip's room, he said, "I wish it would snow for a whole week. Then we wouldn't have to leave until after *Grischtdaag*, and Jane and all Jaala's *groosskinner* could *kumme* over and go sledding with us every day."

"Maybe it will snow enough for them to *kumme* over tomorrow," Fern replied before kissing him on the forehead.

Within minutes, she was snuggled in bed, too, contemplating whether she was doing the right thing by selling Roman's house instead of continuing to live in it with the children. Obviously, Phillip and Patience loved being there. And the main reason Fern had initially been so eager to leave was that she didn't want to live anywhere near Walker. But now that their discord appeared to be resolved, Fern could picture rebuilding a friendship with him.

Actually, if she was being completely honest with herself, she could almost envision rebuilding a romantic relationship with Walker, too. Recalling how she felt when he'd pulled her close in the buggy, Fern shivered for the third time that evening. But whether Walker had felt the same flicker of attraction or not, Fern knew better than to trust a fleeting emotion. And she certainly knew better than to trust *Walker.*

But she *could* trust the Lord. Realizing she'd never prayed about her decision to sell the house, Fern sat up, pulled her prayer *kapp* from the bedpost, covered her head and said, "*Gott*, You've given me this provision and I want to use it wisely, especially for the sake of my *kinner.* Please make Your will about it abundantly clear to me. And please help me to know whether to guard my heart or open it concerning Walker, too. *Denki*, Lord."

Fern was about to say amen and slide beneath the quilt, when she added, "If You're willing, please let it snow enough for the *kinner* to go sledding tomorrow."

Jane was sleeping by the time they got home, so instead of waking her, Walker carried her into the house and upstairs to her bed. Allowing her to sleep in her clothes, he removed her shoes and piled two quilts on top of her before tiptoeing to his own room.

Once in bed, he pressed his hands against his belly in an attempt to soothe its agitation. *I shouldn't have eaten so much*, he thought, even though he knew that wasn't really why his stomach was in knots. It was his feelings about Fern that were wreaking havoc on his insides. Being with her tonight reminded him of the past they'd once shared. And thinking about their past stirred a yearning to share a future with her, too.

But that was crazy. Even if Fern felt the

same inclination toward him, Walker was only too aware that he could never tell her why he married Gloria. Nor could he ever keep a secret about something as important as that from a woman he seriously courted. Just as importantly, Fern had a history of quickly redirecting her affections. *How could I be sure she wouldn't do that again? What if I told her my secret and gave her my heart again and she suddenly decided she preferred Stephen as a suitor?*

Reining in his wild imagination, Walker reminded himself his emotions would be easier to manage after Fern was gone. He'd only have to see her one more time before she left Serenity Ridge, and now that Roman had died, there was no reason she'd ever need to return again. The thought should have calmed him, but Walker's stomach was gripped with a spasm. He moaned as he rolled onto his side, recalling what Patience had whispered into his ear at the pizza parlor.

"If I had a *daed*, I'd want him to be just like you," she'd said. Walker understood her wistfulness, because deep down, in spite of everything, if he had a wife, he'd *still* want her to be just like Fern.

Chapter Nine

It was flurrying when Fern and the children woke up. Phillip gobbled up his eggs on toast and Patience finished hers almost as quickly so they could be dressed—this time Fern insisted Phillip wear his hat—and waiting outside for their cousin to arrive. Fern came outside with them, as she wanted to determine whether it was too cold to hang the clothes she'd washed on the line. There was a breeze, so they might dry if she hung them out here, but they also might freeze. If she hung them in the basement, they might still be damp by the time they left tomorrow—if they left tomorrow.

While she stood there trying to make up her mind, Walker's buggy approached, and Patience and Phillip zoomed across the lawn to greet them. Walker brought the horse to a halt and helped Jane down from the carriage before retrieving a red plastic sled from the back, which he handed to her.

"Look what I brought!" Jane announced, pulling the sled by its rope.

"Oh, *gut*, now we don't have to use a bin cover," Patience said. She'd been apprehensive ever since Fern told her that's how she and Gloria used to go sledding when they were teenagers.

"I'm still going to use a bin cover," Phillip declared. "I want to spin on my way down the hill."

"You're not going to get very far on the sled yet—the ground is barely coated," Fern cautioned, but the three children optimistically dashed off to take a trial run down the big hill behind the house.

As Walker came nearer, a tickle rippled down Fern's spine, just as it had the previous evening. How was it the very sight of him coming toward her with his long, determined stride could make her feel this way when last Saturday she hadn't been able to glance sideways at him? Studying him now, she noticed his face was blanched despite the brisk air. "You look like you could use some tea, Walker. Would you like to *kumme* in?"

He chortled. "Is that your way of telling me I look tired?"

"Frankly, I actually think you look nauseated," Fern said, not unkindly. "Tea always settles my *bauch*."

"*Denki*, but I'll be all right." He patted his stomach. "I admit my eyes were bigger than my *bauch* last night, but I couldn't let Phillip show me up."

"Oh, then your eyes were bigger than *Phillip's* stomach," Fern jested, and

Walker chuckled. She had always liked making him laugh. When they were courting she claimed it made his eyes greener, which made him laugh even louder. "*Denki* again for a memorable evening. I'm so glad we didn't miss looking at the lights together. I haven't had that much fun since..." Fern couldn't remember the last time she'd had that much fun. It was probably one of the last times she went out with Walker before she left Serenity Ridge. But she couldn't say that, so she said, "Since Jane's *Grischtdaag* program." *At least, it was* schpass *up until our argument.*

"I enjoyed it, too. A lot," Walker emphasized, pushing the brim of his wool hat upward so he could peer into her eyes. Or so she could peer into his. *Sea green*, she once called them, even though she'd never seen the sea. One of the girls squealed in the backyard and Walker broke off his gaze and tipped his head toward the sky. "I haven't spoken to anyone about the forecast yet, but if this keeps up, I have a hunch you won't be leaving tomorrow."

"I know two *kinner*—no, make that *three kinner* who would be very *hallich* about that, especially if it meant we had to stay into next week."

"I know one adult who'd be *hallich* about that, too," Walker said. Fern's heart skittered. What did he mean by that? It seemed forever before he added, "Jane is going to be very weepy when you go and right now, I'm on my own to console her. So the longer you stay, the better."

Fern's hope melted as quickly as the snowflakes that landed on Walker's beard. She surprised herself by thinking, *I might be weepy when we go, too.* "I think I have it worse," she joked. "I'm on my own to console *two* sad *kinner.*"

"No one's forcing you to leave so soon," he said, grinning. Was he indicating he wanted her to stay, or was he just reminding her it didn't matter to him whether they sold the house or she lived in it for a while?

Fern vaguely responded, "I wonder what the policy is for changing my bus tickets in the event of a storm."

"If you'd like, I can take you to the phone shanty this afternoon so you can call to find out."

"*Denki*, I'd appreciate that." Walker was so helpful; Fern was going to miss that. Adam was helpful, too, but in a general way. When Walker offered to help with something, Fern felt as if he really wanted to do it, and he wanted to do it specifically for her. It made her feel...well, it made her feel special.

After he left, Fern realized since it was snowing harder now, if she hung the clothes on the line, they'd get wet as well as frozen, and they'd have virtually no chance of drying. If she hung them in the basement, they probably wouldn't dry, but at least they'd be less damp than they were now. So she set the basket back on the porch, thinking, *I wish my decision about selling the* haus *was that easy to make.*

Before going inside, she ambled around to the backyard to check on the children. There were several stripes of brown earth stretching down the hill from where they'd worn a path through the snow to the ground. Jane and Patience were together on the sled, and the snow was so sparse they kept getting stuck and had to nudge themselves forward with their hands. Although the incline was relatively steep, there was a long, flat stretch of yard at the bottom, which meant that even if they picked up speed on their descent, the girls would come to a gradual stop at the end of their ride. Fern decided it would be safe for the children to sled alone while she did the breakfast dishes, since she could see them from the kitchen window.

She was turning to leave when Phillip warned the girls to get out of his way. Fern glanced back and saw him beginning to descend the hill while standing on the trash bin lid.

"Absatz!" she shouted, and he immediately hopped off the lid. "I don't want you standing on that to go down the hill. You could break a bone!" Then, so there'd be no question about her instructions, she added, "I don't want you standing up on the sled, either. You can go on your bottom only."

"Can't I go on my knees?" the boy bargained.

"Jah, but only face forward," she allowed.

"What if I start out going face forward but I spin around and end up going face backward? Should I roll off?"

"Neh, if that happens, don't roll off. Hang on for dear life!" On second thought, Fern wondered if she ought to forbid Phillip to go down the hill on his knees. As Walker said, he was athletic, so she didn't want to hinder his abilities by being overly protective. Nor did she want him to get

hurt. She wished that Walker hadn't left yet; he would have had a better sense of what kind of limits to put on Phillip's rambunctious stunts.

After an additional warning to the children to be careful, Fern went inside and washed, dried and put away the dishes, monitoring the trio from the window. By the time she finished tidying the kitchen, they'd moved on to making patterns in the snow with their boots.

Fern darted downstairs to clip the clothes to the line strung from one beam of the ceiling to the other. The rope was so frayed she didn't know if it would hold. *Roman has probably been using the same clothesline since I lived here.* She couldn't imagine him doing his own laundry, yet at the far end of the line hung a shirt and a pair of Roman's trousers. Whether he or one of the women who'd cleaned the house pinned them there, Fern didn't know, but she hadn't been able to make herself take them down.

Roman had been a difficult man in many regards; he was exacting, sanctimonious and frugal to an extreme. He never once expressed gratitude for Fern's help when he was alive, which was why it was so surprising he bequeathed the house to her, and not solely to Jane. *He must have appreciated and cared about me after all. Maybe he knew how much I was struggling financially, but for whatever reason, it seems he really wanted me to* live *here.* As she contemplated her uncle's uncharacteristic generosity, Fern again questioned whether she was doing the right thing by selling the house.

Footsteps overhead interrupted her thoughts. She pinned Phillip's last sock to the line and scurried upstairs to make sure that whatever child had just come in had taken off their boots. *I guess there's a little of Roman in me, too,* she mused, chuckling to herself.

It was actually Jaala who was standing in the living room, saying she knocked but

Fern didn't answer so she had to let herself in before she turned into an icicle. The older woman told Fern that Abram had dropped her and her three eldest grandchildren there on his way to a doctor's appointment. "We came by last night but you weren't here and I was afraid you'd left ahead of the storm. I would have been sorry if I'd missed you."

"I would have been sorry, too, although I'm concerned about all of you traveling in this weather. How are the roads?"

"It's barely starting to stick, so we'll make it home just fine, *Gott* willing." Jaala extended a rectangular container to Fern. "A few slices for your journey—or for dessert tonight, if your travel plans are delayed."

"Oh, *denki*!" Fern didn't have to lift the lid to know Jaala's scrumptious spice cake with cream cheese frosting was inside. "That was so thoughtful of you. Would you like a piece of it with tea? I'm afraid my cupboards are bare, since I thought we'd be leaving."

"*Neh*, save the cake for you and the *kinner*. But I would like tea." Jaala hung her coat, scarf and winter bonnet on an empty peg on the wall. "When Abram returns, he can take you to the store and then *kumme* back for us. I'll stay with the *kinner*. Otherwise, you might be stuck here without anything to eat but cake."

"Phillip would love that!" Fern laughed. "But you don't need to take me to the store. You live so far away and I don't want to keep you from getting home as soon as you can. Walker is returning shortly for Jane and he's bringing me to the phone shanty, so it's not that much farther for us to go into town from there." *I just hope I brought enough money to purchase food for the few extra days...*

Jaala reluctantly accepted Fern's decision. "If the storm prevents you from leaving before *Grischtdaag*, you must spend the holiday with us. We'll *kumme* get you.

As I said, the more the merrier. Which reminds me, I heard Louisa had to leave because Willa and her *kinner* were sick. I must be sure to invite Walker and Jane for *Grischtdaag*, too."

Oh, that would be schpass! Fern briskly retreated to the kitchen so Jaala wouldn't see her lips dancing upward with giddy hopefulness. After the tea was ready, the two women chatted for another hour, and Jaala graciously agreed to help Walker organize an estate sale if the agent or home buyer didn't want to acquire Roman's possessions.

"You and Abram should take whatever items you want, first," Fern told her. The deacon and his wife unfailingly shared everything they had with those in need, including Fern, so it was a pleasure to be able to give back to them for once.

When they heard heavy footsteps on the porch, Fern's pulse quickened, wondering whether it was Abram or if Walker had returned early. To her dismay, it turned out to be Stephen.

"I brought two of my nephews over to go sledding," he explained after Fern grudgingly invited him in. He greeted Jaala before continuing, "I also wanted to see if there's anything you need before the storm sets in. This morning an *Englischer* in town told me we're going to get up to twenty inches overnight and it's already awfully slick out there."

Twenty inches! Fern swallowed a gasp. There wasn't any possibility they'd be leaving Serenity Ridge tomorrow and it might be days before the roads were navigable. She knew she couldn't make a box of chocolates, two slices of leftover pizza and a quarter of a spice cake last for that long. Fern glanced out the window; it was snowing much heavier now. While she'd rather go to the market with Walker, she didn't want to put him and Jane in jeopardy by delaying their trip home.

Before Fern could come to a decision,

Jaala answered for her. "Fern's pantry is empty. She needs a ride to the market before the roads get too bad. I'll stay here with the *kinner*. If Abram returns meanwhile, he'll wait with me until you two get back."

Fern didn't even have a chance to refuse; Stephen was practically out the door before Jaala finished speaking. She realized she should be grateful for his willingness to help. No matter how uncomfortable she felt about going with him alone to the market, Fern would feel even worse if the children were housebound without anything to eat. So she reluctantly bundled into her coat and bonnet and followed Stephen's footprints through the snow to his buggy.

Although the road Roman lived on was coated with two to three inches of snow, the main road was comparatively clean, since the passing vehicles had melted wide paths on the pavement. *It would have been fine if I had waited until Walker came back*, Fern grumbled to herself. Suspecting Stephen may have exaggerated the magnitude of the storm in order to have an excuse to stop by Roman's house, she balled her gloved fingers on her lap.

"Don't worry, I won't let anything happen to you." Stephen apparently thought she was nervous, which only irritated Fern more.

She asked him to stop at the phone shanty on the way so she could change her bus tickets. To her relief, because of the impending nor'easter, the transportation company rescheduled her tickets without charging any additional fees, as long as she left on Tuesday's bus. "I tried to warn you to leave this morning," the van driver said when Fern called him. But Fern didn't care; she wouldn't have left this morning no matter what. She hadn't felt ready. She didn't even know if she'd feel ready by Tuesday.

"What's your new departure date?" Stephen asked before she was even seated again.

Fern supposed he was just making friendly conversation, but she resented him asking about her schedule and she replied tersely, "Tuesday morning."

"That means you'll be here on *Grischtdaag*. You're *wilkom* to join us at my *bruder*'s *haus* if you have nowhere else to go."

"*Denki*, but if the roads are passable, I've already told Jaala I'd spend *Grischtdaag* with her *familye*." *And with Walker,* Gott *willing.*

Then it dawned on Fern that even if the roads *were* passable, there was a good chance Walker and Jane would go to Willa's, not to Jaala's, provided Willa's family had recovered. *Unless the Lord gives me a clear indication I shouldn't sell the* haus, *I probably won't see Walker again after he picks Jane up this afternoon.* Fern's chest tightened when she realized she might not even see him *then*. It was possible Walker would return to Roman's house while she was at the market and he'd need to leave for his own home before the roads worsened. *Please* Gott, *don't let that happen*, she silently pleaded.

"I've already sent everyone else home. You ought to leave, too," Levi Swarey told Walker shortly before noon, even though the tree farm was hopping with frantic customers. As the owner of the tree business, Levi lived on the property, so at the end of the day all he had to do was stroll up the driveway to his house. He said he'd be closing the farm shortly anyway, since the roads were getting too bad for the *Englischers* to travel on them.

"But you've got a dozen customers in line to have their trees baled, and who knows how many more are still out in the aisles searching for their trees," Walker argued.

"Otto will help me take care of them." Levi was referring to his brother-in-law, who also worked for him and lived within walking distance. "Go ahead. Be safe and *Frehlicher Grischtdaag.*"

On the way to Fern's house, Walker took a slight detour to stop at the phone shanty closest to Levi's farm, since that was the one Walker and his mother always used, to see if there were any messages for him. Even though he and his mother had arranged to speak the following morning, Walker figured she might have heard the weather report and decided to give him an update while she still could.

His intuition proved right; someone had scrawled a lengthy message from Louisa on the whiteboard. It was marked with today's date and indicated everyone in Willa's family had recovered and was looking forward to seeing Walker and Jane, but Louisa hoped they wouldn't take any chances journeying in inclement weather. The note also mentioned she said he ought to purchase enough food to last him and Jane three days. Walker chuckled at his mother's ability to treat him like a child even long distance. In turn, he left a message for her at the phone shanty in Unity, obediently promising to wait until the roads were safe before going to Unity, and informing her there were enough leftovers in the fridge to keep him and Jane alive for a week.

As he continued toward Fern's house, Walker kept a tight rein on Daisy. Some of the roads had either been sanded or plowed, while others hadn't. It wasn't that the snow was too deep yet—maybe four inches—but the flakes were big and they were falling fast. Every once in a while a gust of wind would blow the precipitation sideways, diminishing Walker's visibility and unsettling Daisy. While he imagined the conditions were going to be even more hazardous by the time he took Fern and the *kinner* to the phone shanty, he hesitated to push his horse faster than she was already moving. *Lord, please protect everyone on the road today and deliver me quickly to Fern's* haus, he prayed without closing his eyes.

Then he realized he'd been thinking of Roman's house as Fern's, even though she apparently had no intention of making it hers. That morning he'd told her how much he enjoyed being with her again. And, despite being fully aware of all the reasons it would be better for both of them if she left, he even hinted that she should reconsider staying, but she'd acted as if she hadn't heard. *I suppose I ought to be glad—at least that means she isn't interested in staying here to pursue a courtship with Stephen.*

Or so he thought, until he arrived at Fern's house and learned from Jaala and Abram that Stephen had stopped by with his nephews and he'd taken Fern to the phone shanty and market so she could stock up on groceries before the storm.

"We expected them back some time ago," Jaala said, her forehead stitched with lines.

Abram placed his hand over his wife's. "I think they're fine, but let's ask *Gott* to protect them and all the other people out on the road."

The three of them had just finished praying together when the children clamored onto the porch.

"*Kumme* watch us sledding, *Daed*," Jane pleaded when Walker opened the door. Her skin around her mouth was bright red; she'd been licking her mittens again.

"I'm cold," one of Jaala's grandchildren whined. "And *hungerich*."

"You should take your *groosskinner* home. You live farther away than I do," Walker insisted to Jaala and Abram. "I'll stay with the other *kinner*."

It took some persuading, but Jaala eventually relented. Before she left, she told Walker, "You and Jane are invited to spend *Grischtdaag* with us if you don't head off to Unity. And please remind Fern now that she's staying, I expect her for

Grischtdaag. Abram will *kumme* get her in the morning, won't you, Abram?"

"Of course." The deacon nodded and clapped Walker on the shoulder. "If we don't see you on the twenty-fifth, have a *Frehlicher Grischtdaag* with your *fami-lye*."

Walker followed Abram and Jaala out onto the porch. Abram apparently had cleared the drive at least once because there was only a dusting of snow on it and his buggy rolled along with ease. After the couple departed, Walker went around to the backyard and watched and waved as the children took turns sailing down the hill on an assortment of sleds. Although he occasionally clapped and cheered them on, his mind was on Fern and Stephen.

Once again, she'd opted to go with him when she'd made plans to go with Walker. But this time, he knew he had no reason to be angry. Fern likely had chosen to go with Stephen because the weather was getting worse, and she thought it would be too risky to wait until Walker returned before heading out in it. Jaala was there to watch the children, so the timing must have seemed perfect. Fern's decision to ride with Stephen likely had nothing to do with her having a romantic interest in him.

Yet in spite of logically understanding Fern's motives, Walker still felt utterly deflated because he kept circling back to the same conclusion: as much fun as he'd had with Fern and hoped she'd stay in Serenity Ridge, Walker could never tell her about Jane. He could never marry her. The closest he'd ever come to being her husband— or even her suitor—was taking her out to an ice cream parlor or sharing supper with their children. That wasn't enough for him. And if she felt any romantic inclination for him, it wouldn't be enough for her, either. No, it was better if she left.

And it was better if he put his mind on other things. Telling the children he'd be in the front yard, Walker retrieved the ax from the barn. The logs were covered in snow and the chopping block was slippery, so he gave up after only a few attempts. *I hope Fern and Stephen are okay*, he thought as he went back to the barn to put the ax away.

When he emerged, he saw them slogging from Stephen's parked buggy toward the house, each hugging a paper bag of groceries, their heads bent against the wind and snow. Stephen noticed Walker first and gave him a wave. Then Fern lifted her head.

"Walker!" she exclaimed. "I'm so sorry you had to wait for us. There was an accident on Laurel Lane and we waited forever for traffic to clear, only to be detoured to the other side of town because they closed Grove Street completely. I feel *baremlich* you've had to stay here with the *kinner*. When did Jaala and Abram leave?"

"A while ago, but it's okay, I don't mind. I'm just glad the two of you are all right," Walker answered, feeling guilty she was so distressed. *After how I reacted last time she got a ride from Stephen, it's no wonder.* Taking the bag from her arms and motioning for Stephen to give him the other one, he added, "I'll place these inside the door and then I should be on my way."

"So should I." Stephen started around toward the back of the house to call his nephews, but Fern hung back, waiting for Walker to set the groceries inside before heading for the backyard. Stephen had already summoned his nephews and they were running toward him, dragging their sleds behind them. He directed the children to say goodbye to Fern and Walker, and then he touched Fern's shoulder. "I hope this isn't the last time I get to see you."

"Goodbye, Stephen," was Fern's simple reply, but Walker noticed she took a step backward, closer to him than to Stephen. Once they left, Walker beckoned to Jane, too.

"We have to go already?" she whined loudly from the top of the hill.

"*Jah*, the roads are getting dangerous. We need to skedaddle."

"Aww," Jane grumbled. She appeared to be on the brink of tears. "Can't we just go down three more times? Please, *Daed*?"

"Okay," he relented. "Three more times if you go together. Or one more time each if you go separately."

They chose to go together, so they'd each get three more turns. The snow was packed down where they'd been sledding and their combined weight increased their momentum, so they whizzed down the hill. Since Phillip was in front, a spray of snow coated his face, and when they came to a stop a few yards in front of where Walker and Fern were standing, he rolled off the sled and mugged. "Look, I've got a beard like you'll have when you're an old man, Walker."

Walker doubled over and Fern did, too. By the time they'd stopped laughing, the children had plodded to the top of the hill again. This time it was Jane's turn in the front. Watching them position themselves on the sled, Fern remarked, "Jaala said we're invited for *Grischtdaag* if we're both stuck in town."

"*Jah*, she told me that, too. She said Abram's picking you up in the morning. But I stopped at the phone shanty and my *mamm* left a message that Willa's *familye* is well again. So as soon as the roads are travelable, we'll leave for Unity."

"Oh, well, I'm glad your *schwesder* and her *kinner* feel better." Fern wrapped her arms around herself. "Jaala also said she'd help organize an estate sale for Roman's belongings."

"I'd appreciate that. My *mamm* will help too, I'm sure. And I'll finish the shingles on the roof and clean up the rest of the yard after *Grischtdaag*."

"I can't tell you how much I appreciate all you've done for me—for all three of us," Fern said, a catch in her voice.

Walker couldn't look at her for fear he'd choke up. "I was glad to do it."

"The *kinner* will want to write each other, and who knows, maybe we'll visit Serenity Ridge some time and they'll see each other then."

"Or we'll have a reason to go to Ohio and our paths will cross there," Walker said, although he knew neither scenario was likely.

For the children's final run down the hill, Patience was supposed to sit in the front, but she must have opted out, because Phillip was first and it looked like Jane's arms that were wrapped around his torso from behind. Patience was obscured behind her. The children whooped the entire way down the hill. Hearing their elation, it occurred to Walker that was how exhilarating the past week was, too—and how soon it was over.

All five of them trudged to the barn together, with Phillip carrying the sled upside down on his head. Walker had wheeled the buggy inside so he could hitch Daisy to it without the animal being unnerved by the swirling snow.

When he was finished, he took the sled from Phillip, and Fern said, "We'll send you our address when we get to Ohio so you can write to us, Jane."

"But how can we leave when it's snowing so much?" Phillip questioned.

"We aren't leaving today, but this is the last time we'll see Jane and Walker," Fern explained. "They're going to Unity for *Grischtdaag*. Jane's other *gschwischderkinner* are excited they get to see her."

"*I'm* excited *I* get to see her, too," Phillip groused.

"I know, but *Gott* gave us a blessing by allowing us to spend this week together, and instead of asking for more, we ought to be grateful for the *schpass* we had," Fern exhorted her son, and Walker glumly supposed he ought to take her admonishment to heart, too. "It's time to say goodbye so Walker and Jane can get home safely."

Phillip wrapped his arms around his cousin's waist so tightly he practically lifted her off the ground. When he let go, Jane hugged Patience, who, oddly, was the only child smiling. "*Denki* for sharing your sled, Jane," she said. "Next time, I might try going in the front."

Fern bent over and kissed Jane on the cheek before embracing her tightly, and Walker also crouched down to give Phillip and Patience a hug. When he straightened, he and Fern looked at each other, as if not sure what to do. They both stretched out their arms at the same time and moved forward for a quick embrace, but Walker bumped his chin against the stiff brim of Fern's bonnet and he jerked backward, so then they just squeezed each other's hands instead.

"Goodbye, Walker." Although a scarf covered Fern's eyes and nose, Walker saw that her sterling-colored eyes were blurred with tears, whether from the cold or from emotion, he wasn't sure.

His voice gravelly, Walker uttered, "Goodbye, Fern."

Then he and Jane climbed into the buggy and started down the driveway. Although he'd given her the option of sitting up front with him, she wanted to sit in the back, and Walker could hear that she was trying to stifle her sobs, just as he was trying to keep his own emotions in check.

It might have been better if they had never kumme, *rather than to see Fern again and have Jane meet the* kinner *and then go through the pain of separation. And the knowledge of what we're missing,* he thought as he journeyed homeward. Since Fern indicated Grove Street was closed, Walker had to take a side road that was straighter but less heavily trafficked than the main road.

As soon as he turned onto it, he realized a plow was headed in their direction. Walker didn't have time to bring the animal to a stop, so he directed Daisy to the side of the road, but it was no use: the plow's flashing lights and rumbling sound spooked her and she bolted.

"Daed!" Jane exclaimed, but Walker couldn't comfort her. He had to focus on halting the horse. In the blowing snow, he could hardly tell which way was up and which way was down, much less which side of the road they were on. But when the buggy began to jostle so hard he lost his hat, Walker knew they were no longer on the pavement at all.

"Daed!" Jane screamed again, louder this time. "Make her stop!"

Chapter Ten

Once Fern put away the groceries, she made hot chocolate—she'd purchased a canister of cocoa as a Christmas treat—and carried three mugs on a tray into the living room, where the children were snuggled under quilts on the sofa.

"We get to drink that in here?" Patience asked.

"*Jah*, we'll be careful," Fern said as she situated herself in between the two children and handed them each a mug and a napkin. Usually Fern made them sit at the kitchen table to eat or drink anything, but after the children had spent so much time outdoors, they were chilled to the bone. "I want to keep you as close to the wood-stove as possible so you won't catch colds. The last thing I want is for you to have to travel on Tuesday when you're sick."

"I don't want to have to travel at *all*," Phillip complained. "I like it here."

Rather than reminding her son a second time that it wasn't appreciative to ask the Lord to give them more time in Serenity Ridge than He'd already given them, Fern admitted, "I like it here, too."

"Then why do we have to leave?"

Because that's what I believe is Gott's *best for us,* Fern thought. But she still wasn't positive. "I've already paid for our bus tickets." Her answer rang hollow, so she added, "And there might be a surprise for us in Ohio, but unless we go back we can't find out what it is."

"What kind of a surprise? Is it a *Grischtdaag* present?" Patience asked.

Fern had actually been alluding to securing a home of their own, but Patience's question caused her to remember she'd left the children's modest presents at Adam's house, since she thought they'd return by Christmas. "*Jah*, your *Grischtdaag* presents are in Ohio. There might be something else there for you, too."

Phillip didn't seem the least bit curious. Nor was he interested in his hot chocolate. Setting the cup on the surface of the rolling lamp table next to Roman's Bible, he sighed. "I'm too sad to drink my cocoa."

"Don't be sad, Phillip." Patience tipped her head backward to slurp down the rest of her drink. When she finished, she had a brown mustache above her lip. "*Mamm* said I could ask *Gott* to let us use this *haus*. I think He will say *jah*, so we're not going to have to leave."

Now Fern understood why Patience hadn't been at all dismayed about saying goodbye to Jane and Walker; the child had full faith it wasn't the last time they'd see each other. Fern gently tried to disavow her of the notion, saying, "I don't think you should count on that, Patience. But the Lord has given us almost three more days here than we would have gotten if it hadn't snowed. So we ought to show that we're grateful. How would you like to worship in preparation for *Grischtdaag*?"

"I know!" Patience's eyes glimmered. "Let's light the candles and read the verses about Jesus being borned. The ones Jane said at her *Grischtdaag* program."

This got Phillip's attention. He pulled the Bible from the table and handed it to Fern, and then both children cuddled up close to her. She read aloud until she got to the verses Jane had recited at the school and Phillip interrupted, "*Neh*, let me say that part, *Mamm*."

He quoted the verses word for word, amazing Fern, who hadn't realized Jane had had such a positive influence on him, as well as on Patience. After completing the passage, Fern got up and lit the candles, and then they sang four Christmas carols before Phillip announced his stomach was rumbling.

Glad to see he was feeling more like his usual self, Fern said she'd go start supper while they put away their mittens, scarves and socks that had dried in front of the fire. As she measured water into a pot— she was back to serving rice and beans for supper—Fern overheard Phillip ask his sister, "Remember when Walker said Jane's feet *schtinke*?"

"*Jah*, that was *voll schpass*," Patience said with a giggle.

"Smell these."

After a pause, Patience squealed, "Eww! Why do they smell like that?"

"It's because I'm a man and men sweat a lot on their heads and feet. Walker sweats a lot, too."

Fern made a noise that was neither a chuckle nor a sob as she realized this was a trip her children would never forget. *And neither will I*, she thought.

When the meal was nearly prepared, she

turned down the flame beneath the pot of rice and called the children, who by then had gone upstairs to play the card game Jane had forgotten. They sounded like a herd of cattle clamoring down the stairs, so Fern rushed to the living room to see if one of them had taken a tumble. Instead of her children she was startled to find the front door open and Walker standing on the threshold, literally coated in snow, with Jane in his arms. She was wrapped in a blanket and shivering, her eyes closed and her plump cheeks nearly scarlet from the cold.

"Help," he implored. "We went off the road. Jane hit her head on the buggy seat."

That was all the information Fern needed for now. "*Kumme* lay her on the bed. Be very gentle," she directed Walker and led him to Roman's old bedroom. Then she told him to go put a kettle of water on the stove. As she exchanged Jane's wet clothing for one of her own dresses, Fern checked her for any bleeding or additional injuries. All the while, she asked the child questions to assess whether she was having nausea or vision problems. Although Jane's teeth chattered and a large egg had formed on her scalp just above her forehead, to Fern's relief she was cognizant of her surroundings, and it appeared she'd be fine once she warmed up.

"Walker!" she cried, and he was through the door in an instant. "Let's get her onto the sofa by the woodstove."

Walker picked Jane up again, and Fern whisked the quilt and wool blanket from her bed. In the living room, she told Patience and Phillip to fetch their quilts from upstairs. Fern layered those on top of Jane, too, assuring Walker, "She's okay. She's going to be just fine."

He just hovered over his daughter, completely speechless, a grimace distorting his features.

"D-d-daed." Jane's teeth knocked together as she stammered, "Your b-beard is d-d-dripping on me."

Fern chuckled and dabbed the water from Jane's forehead with a corner of the blanket, but Walker still didn't utter a sound. Growing more concerned about him than she was about his daughter, Fern touched his shoulder. "*Kumme*, you're soaking wet. Take off your coat and sit in the rocker by the fire. I saw a pair of my *onkel*'s work clothes in the basement. I'll go get them."

"I—I—I have to put Daisy in the b-b-barn first. Sh-she's tethered to the fence and she's ag-agitated from the snow."

Fern didn't want Walker to go back outside alone in the state he was in; neither did she want to leave Jane just yet. "Phillip can go with you," she said, shooting Phillip a meaningful look. Her young, courageous son gave her a nod, acknowledging he understood.

"*Neh*—" Walker began to object but Phillip cut in.

"I can hold the flashlight," he volunteered, scrambling to put his boots and coat on.

By the time the two went out and came back, Patience had brought Jane a sweater and had managed to put dry wool socks on her feet for her. Jane was sitting upright, sipping the hot chocolate Fern made with the water she'd asked Walker to boil. After Walker had dried off and changed into Roman's old clothes, Fern gave him a cup of tea, but he set it aside and picked up his daughter, settling into the rocking chair with her.

Jane's legs dangled over the arm of the chair and as Fern covered them with the quilt, she noticed the tempestuous look in Walker's eyes. She'd seen that same look only once before, after he'd rescued Phillip from the tree branch. Whatever happened on the road had frightened Walker gravely, but she dared not question him about it. He wasn't ready to talk and she didn't want to upset him further by pushing him. Her children seemed to pick up on her cue—they sat beside Fern in silence as Walker rocked Jane back and forth.

Without realizing she was doing it, Fern began to softly hum. First, a song from the *Ausbund.* Then, a Christmas carol. And another and another until in the middle of the fourth one, Jane announced, "Something smells *gut.* I'm *hungerich.*"

"It's supper," Fern announced brightly. "But I don't think you should eat very much until we're sure your *bauch* is all right. Maybe you can have a little rice, but no beans."

"Aw, I wish I didn't have to eat any of those beans, either," Phillip grumbled, since black beans were one of the few foods he disliked. To Fern's relief, his comment seemed to pull Walker back into the present. He stood Jane upright in front of him and then they all moved into the kitchen.

Although Fern was worried she wouldn't have enough food to satisfy everyone,

Walker hardly ate a bite anyway. He still looked stunned but he told the story, little by little, of how the lights from a snow plow had frightened Daisy and the animal took off into a field, throwing Jane from the seat and nearly tipping the buggy in the process. Walker blindly managed to guide the horse in big circles, so eventually she tired out and wound to a halt. Since the road was infrequently traveled, it was already getting dark and the horse had run herself ragged, Walker unhitched the buggy. Then he pulled Jane on the sled with one hand and led Daisy to Roman's house—the nearest residence—with the other.

When he was done speaking, he tugged at the hair on his chin. His face slipped into a faraway expression again, as if he was literally lost in thought, until Patience patted his shoulder. "I'm *hallich* you and Jane and Daisy are okay," she said. "You must have been sore afraid."

For a moment, Walker just stared

blankly at the little girl, so she added, "That's really, really afraid. So afraid it makes you sore. Like the shepherds in the field with their flocks, except you were in a field with Jane and you didn't see an angel, did you?"

Fern held her breath, half anticipating an emotional outburst from Walker. But he cupped his hand behind Patience's head and drew her toward him to kiss her forehead. "*Neh.* I didn't see an angel, but *Gott* protected us and I'm *hallich* about that, too." He picked up his fork and began eating his rice.

"And I'm *hallich* you get to stay overnight." Phillip pushed a bean to the side of his plate. "You can sleep with me in my room, Walker."

"*Denki*, but I'll sleep in the workshop," Walker asserted and Fern didn't argue with him. She figured he might need space for himself and besides, it didn't seem proper for them to stay overnight in the house without any other adults there.

When they were courting he was as committed to maintaining their reputations and protecting their modesty as she was, and she was relieved he hadn't changed in that regard.

The children were so tired from sledding that they went to bed almost immediately after Fern and Patience washed, dried and put away the supper dishes.

"If you hear something hitting the roof, that's the tree," Patience told her roommate before they headed toward the stairs. "Your *daed* sawed off the branch that used to tap every night but there's a new one that hangs down because it's got heavy snow on it."

"Really?" Fern was surprised. Patience must have noticed the branch rapping against her side of the house that afternoon but she hadn't complained about it.

"*Jah*, but it's okay. Walker said it's just the tree waving its arms to get my attention. It's too sturdy to fall."

Fern caught Walker's eye. "Well, he

knows more about trees than anyone I know," she said with a wink before following the children upstairs to tuck them into bed. When she returned with a stack of blankets, Walker was stoking the fire and he'd filled the wood bin, too. Fern thanked him and asked if he wanted tea. "I plan to bake dessert tomorrow, but for now I can offer you a piece of *kuche* from Jaala. Or one of the chocolates I confiscated from Jane."

Walker's smile belied the sadness in his eyes. Or maybe he was merely exhausted as he said, "I'd better go check on Daisy and then get a fire started in the workshop. So I'll say good-night now."

While he put on his boots and coat, Fern retrieved a couple extra blankets for the horse and a pillow for Walker. She divided the bedding between two oversize canvas bags she'd also found in the linen closet so they'd be easier for him to carry.

Walker reached to take them from her but she wouldn't let go of the handles, forcing him to look her in the eyes. She wasn't sure what she wanted to say. She only knew she didn't want him to leave without expressing how relieved she was that he and Jane were okay. He raised an eyebrow, waiting. Fern opened her mouth but she was still at a loss for words, so she released the handles.

The next thing she knew, Walker had set the bags back down and drew her toward himself so that her cheek pressed into his damp, scratchy wool coat. He hugged her tightly, just as Phillip had embraced his cousin a few hours earlier, nearly lifting her from the floor. And Fern held on just as tightly for what seemed like a long time, but not nearly long enough.

When he let her go, his eyes were misty. "*Denki*, Fern," he said before turning to leave. "Sleep well."

But sleep eluded her, in part because she was vigilant about checking on Jane. But also because Walker's reaction to another near accident emphasized to her how traumatized he must have been by Jordan's death. She again thought of Louisa telling her that Walker hadn't been in his right mind afterward. That he hadn't been in his right mind when he married Gloria, either.

Is this the Lord's way of telling me to keep an open heart toward Walker after all? she wondered. But even if God was showing her that she ought to be more understanding of Walker, that didn't necessarily mean the Lord was guiding her to stay in Maine. Nor did it mean she was meant to have a romantic relationship with Walker, especially since he hadn't directly expressed an interest in her. Not with words anyway. But was the way he embraced her an indication of his feelings for her? Or was it only another reaction to the trauma of the day's events? Fern had no way of knowing, so again she asked the Lord for guidance.

This time she prayed, "*Gott*, if it's Your will for Walker and me to be in a romantic relationship, please have him show me plainly. And if it's not, please let him show me that in a way that's unmistakable, too. *Denki* for keeping him and Jane safe and *denki* for bringing them back for one more day."

With the woodstove burning, Roman's orderly little workshop was actually warmer than Fern's house, which was fortunate because it meant Walker could use most of the blankets as padding beneath him rather than as a covering over him. After he'd fashioned himself a bed, he turned off the flashlight and lay in the dark. His thoughts whirled through his mind just like the wind whistled through the trees.

He couldn't stop thinking about how comforted he'd been by Fern's presence tonight. Not only had she known exactly how to care for Jane—no doubt because she'd tended to so many relatives with various health conditions over the years—but she'd also calmed his frazzled nerves. Just by being at his side, humming as he gathered his thoughts, Fern had helped quiet the pandemonium in his head and slow his sprinting pulse.

Walker's stomach growled. He would have enjoyed having a piece of dessert with Fern, but he didn't trust himself to be alone with her. The way he was feeling tonight, he was only half a sentence away from breaking down and telling her about Jane. About Gloria. About *every-thing*. He'd nearly done it, too, when they were standing near the door and she was looking at him like that... Instead, at the last minute, he'd hugged her, which may have been inappropriate, but she didn't seem to mind. She probably attributed the embrace to his being in shock, and maybe it was.

For several harrowing minutes as Daisy ran pell-mell through the snowy expanse, Walker was certain the buggy was about to overturn and he'd lose his life, or worse—his daughter would lose hers. So it was only natural if he wasn't quite himself tonight. But having acted in haste after Jordan's death, Walker didn't want to do something he'd regret now, like telling Fern about Gloria's pregnancy. He was aware he needed time to recover emotionally from the fright of what had almost happened.

And because of God's grace, he *had* time to recover. He had more time to spend with Fern and her children, too, and he was determined to make the most of it.

Walker slept through the night and to his relief, he didn't even dream, much less suffer any nightmares. A glance out the window told him it was still snowing. Or maybe it had stopped and started again. Walker shuddered; the fire had died out overnight and he couldn't wait to get back inside the house, but first he wanted to check on Daisy. Fortunately, the Fry boys hadn't taken all of the hay from the barn when they took Roman's horse to their house, so there was plenty for the animal to eat, but Walker was concerned her water might have frozen over.

When he opened the door to go outside, he discovered the snow was over two feet high, which made for a laborious trek to the barn. After tending to the horse, he took Roman's snow shovel from the stand where it was neatly positioned with the other types of shovels and rakes. Walker intended to clear paths from the barn to the workshop and from the workshop to the house. But first, he wanted to get inside and have a cup of coffee. Although the snow was fine and powdery, it was deep, so rather than wading through it, Walker had to pick his way across it by lifting each leg high and extending it forward as far as possible with every step. It took him three times as long as usual to reach the house.

"Guder mariye," Fern greeted him with a mug of coffee. Her eyes were as luminous as her smile this morning. "I'm mak-

ing oatmeal. Go sit by the stove—you must be freezing."

"I was toasty warm until the fire died out." Instead of sitting in the rocking chair by the woodstove, once he removed his boots, Walker followed Fern into the kitchen and took a seat. Just as he was about to ask how Jane was, his daughter joined him at the table.

"Hi, *Daed*!" she greeted him, as vibrant as ever. "Did you see all the snow?"

"*See* it? I had to *swim* through it."

"You did?" Phillip had come into the room from down the hall. "How does somebody swim through snow?"

"As quickly as they can. It's really cold!" Walker joked.

Patience was the last one to take a place at the table. *"Guder mariye,"* she mumbled, rubbing her eyes.

Everyone wished her a good morning, too. "You look sleepy." Walker added sympathetically, "It's not easy sharing a bed, is it? I'm glad I've never had to do that."

"I share a bed with my *gschwischder-kind* in Ohio, so I like it. And Jane kept me nice and warm," Patience said with a yawn. "But in Ohio *Mamm* doesn't *kumme* into our room and wake us up with a flashlight to ask us questions."

"I wasn't asking you—I was asking Jane. I wanted to be sure the bump on her head didn't affect her thinking," Fern told her daughter before sitting down and asking Walker to say grace. When he was done thanking the Lord for their food, Fern apologized, "I'm afraid there's not a lot of toast because I need to conserve the flour in case we're snowed in through Monday, but everyone can have as much oatmeal as you want. Phillip, I heated the two leftover slices of pizza for you."

"I get to eat pizza for breakfast?" Phillip marveled. "I wish we had snowstorms every day!"

"You might not wish that after you're

done helping me shovel," Walker joked. He didn't really intend to put the boy to work, but Phillip was dejected after breakfast when Walker said he couldn't help because there was only one shovel. So Walker ended up giving him the same handy plastic bin cover he'd used as a sled to use as a scoop. In the yard the snow came up past Phillip's stomach, and in some places the drifts were so deep he all but disappeared when he hopped into them, yet the sky showed no signs of stopping.

Because of the bump on Jane's head, Fern didn't want her to overexert herself, so she kept both girls inside. After a couple of hours, Walker sent Phillip inside, too, but he continued to work until lunchtime, carving paths to the barn and workshop and clearing half of the driveway, as well.

A delicious aroma filled his nostrils when he opened the door. "That smells *appenditlich*."

"It's chocolate *kuche*," Jane told him. "Fern did something secret while she was making them."

"I know what the secret is," Phillip taunted. "*Mamm* warmed the cookie sheets."

Patience set her brother straight, jeering, "*Neh*, that's not it. She made them with love."

"Patience, you just told the secret!" Jane's exasperation caused Patience's cheeks to redden.

"It's okay, Patience," Walker comforted her. "Anyone who knows your *mamm* knows she puts love into everything she does."

Now *Fern's* cheeks went pink and Walker regretted his comment. It was truly how he felt about her, but he hadn't meant to voice the thought. She addressed the children instead of him, but there was a lilt in her voice as she said, "It's easy to put love into something you're making for people you care about so much."

Walker blushed so hard he could practically feel the snow evaporating from his damp hair and beard. Was she flirting with him? Even if she had been, Walker understood nothing would come of it, but he liked imagining on some level they still shared a mutual attraction. After lunch he whistled as he ambled back outside and got to work again.

By the time he'd come in for the evening, it was barely flurrying. Inside, he found the children somberly sitting on the sofa, three in a row, like birds on a wire. "Where's your *mamm*?"

"In the bedroom. She's crying."

Walker's heartbeat quickened. "Crying? Why?"

"Phillip broke her teacup," Jane tattled.

"I didn't break it—you and Patience broke it when you pulled the box away. *I* was the one who found it."

"We wanted to see it, too. You should have shared," Patience argued.

Walker gave them each a turn to tell him

what happened. He learned that Phillip found a box hidden beneath a floorboard in Gloria's old room. The box contained two teacups wrapped in packing paper but when the children scuffled over their find, one of the teacups dropped to the floor and the handle broke off. Fern came in and when she saw the broken china, she burst into tears—big, loud tears, according to Patience—and grabbed the teacup and box and ran downstairs. The children followed her but she told them she needed to be alone.

Realizing the teacups must have been the same ones Fern had given Gloria when they were young, Walker groaned and sank into the armchair as the children continued to quibble over who was at fault. Finally, he held up his hand and raised his voice. "It doesn't matter who did what or how the teacup was broken. It was an accident. Nobody meant for it to happen. What's important is that Phillip and Patience's *mamm* is sad right now.

Those teacups were very special to her. Sometimes, when you make someone sad, instead of saying how or why something happened, the best thing you can do is say you're sorry and ask for their forgiveness."

Walker hadn't noticed Fern had crept into the room until Phillip glanced toward the doorway. Walker immediately jumped to his feet in concern. Her eyes were pink-rimmed and her nostrils were, too, but she gave him a weak smile.

"I'm sorry, *Mamm*," Patience said, sniffling.

"Me, too." The knob on Jane's forehead was even more pronounced because she was crimping her brow.

"I'm *very* sorry." Phillip shook his head remorsefully. "I wish I'd never found those teacups."

"Will you forgive us, *Mamm*? Please?" Patience wailed.

Fern swept across the room and crouched in front of the children, her hands on Patience's knees. "Of course I forgive you.

All of you. And do you know why?" she asked. When they didn't answer, she told them, "Because if you really love someone, you forgive them when they ask you to, just as *Gott* forgives us. Forgiveness is a very important way of showing love."

Phillip jumped up and flung his arms around his mother's stomach, knocking her off balance. She caught herself on her palms, and then Patience and Jane knelt to embrace from both sides and she fell the rest of the way onto her bottom. Fern laughed and tipped her head backward to grin up at Walker. "Hugs are an important way to show forgiveness, too," she quipped.

"C'mon, *kinner*, give Fern some air," Walker ordered after a couple minutes, and the children released their grip on her. He reached to help Fern into a standing position but she was so light that when he pulled her up she lost her balance. As he grasped her other shoulder to steady her, their eyes met. He could have stood there with one hand holding hers, the other resting on her upper arm, until Christmas if it weren't that the children were standing there watching them.

Fern blinked twice before slowly stepping away and announcing it was time for supper. Although she apologized again for the modest portions of carrots and macaroni and cheese for the main meal, she said there were plenty of cookies and Jaala's spice cake for dessert.

As they were eating their sweets, Walker broke the news to the children that the next morning after they held their Sunday worship services together, he was going to take Daisy back to the field where he'd abandoned the buggy, so he could shovel it out and then return to Roman's house to pick up Jane.

As expected, the children bellyached about not being able to celebrate Christmas with each other. But Fern came up with an idea to distract them; she suggested they could all make gifts for each other to open on Christmas morning. "It will make us feel like we're still together."

"How can we make gifts? We don't have enough supplies," Phillip countered.

"We won't make *actual* gifts," Fern explained. "See, with gifts it's the thought that counts. So we'll think about what we'd give each other if we could give anything in the world. Then we'll write down what that is—or we'll draw a picture of it—on a piece of paper."

Patience was all for the idea. "We can fold them up and tie them with a ribbon, just like a present."

Delighted with the idea, the children claimed separate parts of the room where they could work on their gifts without anyone else seeing them. Fern cut a couple paper bags into sections and distributed them along with pencils and some lengths of twine she'd found in a drawer in the kitchen. Walker was surprised when she handed him four pieces of paper and as many pieces of string. He hadn't expected the adults would play this game, too, but it was fun trying to think of the gifts he'd most like to give to everyone.

Choosing Phillip's present was easy: a very fast horse. He'd give Patience a dress that wasn't a hand-me-down, although Walker suspected she genuinely preferred clothing that belonged to someone else first. Jane had nearly outgrown her yellow scooter, but he'd actually gotten her a new one this Christmas and didn't want to repeat himself, so he drew a box of loopy straws.

Walker studied Fern as she chewed on the eraser of her pencil. She was always so thoughtful about others, even when playing a game. It was one of the many qualities he'd always valued in her. In that instant, Walker knew exactly what he would give her if he could: the truth. It took all of his willpower to suppress the impulse to write, "I never loved Gloria— or any other woman. I've only ever loved you. I still do. Even though you didn't truly love me as much as you said you did. And even though you didn't love me as much as I loved you." Instead he jotted, *A half gallon of ice cream from Brubaker's.* Then he sighed and Fern glanced up, first at him and then at the clock.

"It's almost bedtime," she told the children. They pleaded with her for a few more minutes to finish with their gift ideas, and then she and Walker both helped them fold and tie the papers. Then they used clothespins to fasten their "gifts" to the twine Fern looped around the staircase until it was time for Walker and Jane to take theirs home with them.

While the children were putting on their pajamas, Fern offered to make tea. This time, Walker didn't refuse, rationalizing that it was his last night with Fern and he'd made it this long without divulging his secret—or his secret feelings—so he could last a couple more hours.

"It's my turn to tuck in the *kinner,*" he said, as if taking turns putting the children to bed was part of a long-established domestic routine.

When Walker turned off the lamp in Phillip's room, the boy said, "Maybe tomorrow when you get back, I can show you how to go down the hill on the trash bin cover. It's a lot of *schpass*."

"I'd like that. *Gut nacht*, Phillip. *Denki* for your help today."

Walker paused outside the girls' room. He thought they were already asleep until he heard Jane say, "I wish my *daed* would marry your *mamm*."

Walker caught his breath to hear his daughter express the longing he'd been wrestling with for the past few days. He stood perfectly still, straining to hear Patience's response.

"Shh!" she cautioned and for a moment, Walker thought she'd sensed he was in the hallway listening to them. Then she explained, "My *mamm* said not to talk like that."

"Why not?"

"She said it's nonsense because two people have to love each other specially to get married." There was a pause before Patience sleepily added, "But your *daed* is our friend."

Utterly dejected, Walker edged toward the staircase. It *was* nonsense to imagine Fern had any romantic feelings toward him. And it was past time for him to put the notion—and himself—to bed.

Chapter Eleven

Fern didn't understand why Walker suddenly changed his mind about staying for tea, but now that he'd left, she didn't feel like having any, either. She removed the kettle from the burner, turned the burner off and went to her room. After she'd put on her nightgown, she settled into a sitting position on her bed and pulled the box from her nightstand onto her lap. She opened it and gently removed the teacup with the broken handle. This was the one she had always used; it was adorned with red tulips. Gloria's tulips were yellow.

Fern had assumed when Gloria got married and moved into Walker's house, she had taken all of her possessions with her. So she was shocked to learn Phillip had found the china beneath a floorboard under the carpet where Gloria used to hide the things she didn't want Roman to find when she lived here. When Fern had realized the handle was broken, she'd burst into sobs as if her heart had fragmented, too, and shut herself up in her room, no doubt frightening the children with her uncharacteristic behavior. But when she'd regained control of her emotions, Fern examined the cup and saw it could be repaired with a little glue. As she was gingerly replacing the china within its bed of packing paper, Fern had found a note and she'd realized prior to marrying Walker, her cousin must have intended to send her the cups, but she'd either forgotten about them or changed her mind.

Now, Fern unfolded the message to read it again.

Dear Fern,

I can imagine it will be very hurtful for you to find out I'm marrying Walker and I'm so sorry about causing you pain.

You told me once there was nothing that could separate us from the love of God in Christ and there was nothing I could do that would be so awful He wouldn't forgive me. I believe that but it doesn't mean I'm not ashamed.

And it doesn't mean you shouldn't be angry with me, either, because you have every right to be. In time, I hope you'll come to forgive me. Knowing you like I do, I think you will. It's my fondest dream our children might share a little bit of the closeness we shared as cousins. As friends.

But even if you stay angry at me forever, I will never stop loving you. Your Gloria

When she'd first read the letter, Fern felt stung that Gloria expressed regret about hurting her, without actually saying she was sorry for marrying Walker. If she had been so ashamed, why did she go ahead and do it anyway? But upon a second and third reading, Fern's resentment dissipated and in its place, a profound sense of remorse filled her heart. She realized that while God had enabled her to let go of much of the bitterness she'd harbored toward Gloria and Walker, she was stubbornly clinging to a little shred of it. If she'd really loved her cousin and her former suitor—and if she really loved *Gott*—as much as she claimed to love them, it was time for her to show it. It was time for her to entirely forgive them for what they'd done in the past.

Surely, this is Gott's *prompting*, Fern thought. She was less certain about what God's answers were to her other questions, the ones about whether she ought to stay in Maine or if she and Walker had a romantic future together. That's why she was so delighted when he said he'd stay for tea—she'd desperately wanted to talk to him. But then he'd changed his mind and went back to the workshop. Time was running out; if Fern was going to stop Anthony from putting the house up for sale, she'd have to act soon.

Dear Lord, she prayed, *please give me the opportunity to speak privately with Walker tomorrow.* She removed her prayer *kapp*, slid the box under her bed and pulled the quilt up to her chin, wondering how she'd broach the topic of courtship. She had just about drifted to sleep when inspiration struck. Fern got out of bed and tiptoed to the staircase to retrieve the Christmas "gift" she'd made for Walker. She had written that she'd like to give him an extra large container of peanut brittle. She took a new piece of paper and wrote, "If I could give you anything in the world, I'd give you my heart, but I can't because it's already yours and only yours." After folding the note and tying a bow around it with twine, she brought it to her room, so she could give it to him in person if it seemed appropriate once they began talking.

But the next morning immediately after they'd worshipped together and enjoyed a light brunch, Walker announced he needed to head out to get the buggy. Fern didn't understand why he was so eager to leave; he and Jane wouldn't travel to Unity until tomorrow anyway, since today was the Sabbath.

Phillip asked if he could go with him, but Walker curtly said it was too far and he didn't want Phillip to slow him down. He must have caught the disappointment clouding Phillip's face, because he added, "The *meed* need your help navigating through the backyard, since you know where the biggest snowdrifts are."

Because she was still concerned about the bump on Jane's head and wanted to keep an eye on her, Fern followed the children outside. They shuffled through the snow to the top of the hill, using their legs to etch a rough path, and then Fern shuffled back down the same way she came, to clear away even more of the fine white powder.

After watching them sled—and, in Phillip's case, *roll*—down the hill for well over an hour, Fern heard someone near the side of the house call her name. *That can't be Walker already*, she thought, just as Stephen clumped into view.

After Fern greeted him he said, "I came to clear your driveway for you but it looks as if someone beat me to it."

"*Jah*, Walker did it." She gestured toward Jane on the hill. "He and Jane went off the road on Friday night and their *gaul* was so tired and spooked they had to leave the buggy in a field and trek all the way back during the storm. Walker is out retrieving it now."

"Walker stayed here overnight?" Stephen raised his brows.

"*Jah*. Both Walker and Jane."

Stephen shook his head, clucking his

tongue against his teeth. "I'm surprised at you, Fern—not at Walker, but at you."

Fern lowered her voice so it wouldn't carry up the hill to the children. "What is *that* supposed to mean?" But she knew exactly what he meant, so before he could respond she growled, "For your information, Walker slept in the workshop."

Stephen shrugged. "I believe you, but, you know, given what happened with Gloria, you should guard your reputation better."

What happened with Gloria? "I have no idea what you're talking about."

"Oh, that's right. You weren't here when her baby was born. Her eight-and-a-half-pound premature baby. They never made a confession to the *kurrich*, but..." Stephen let his implication hang in the air.

For a moment Fern thought she'd gone blind with rage at Stephen, but once she blinked she realized it was just the effect of the sun against the snow. Using all her concentration to temper her response, she intoned, "I'd like you to leave. And don't *kumme* back until you can talk like a gentleman."

Storming away, she shouted to the children, telling them she needed to go warm up for a few minutes. Once inside the house, she filled a glass at the kitchen sink but her hand was trembling too severely to lift it to her mouth. *I don't believe it. Walker wouldn't do something like that and neither would Gloria.* But the more she thought about her cousin's note, the more Fern suspected maybe *this* was what Gloria had been ashamed of doing. Suddenly, everything made sense and nothing made sense at all. *How can this be?*

Fern didn't know how long she stood like that, staring out the window but not really seeing the children fly down the hill on their sleds. When the front door opened and Walker came into the kitchen, she was still wearing her coat and clutching the water glass. He told her Abram happened to be passing as he was shoveling the buggy out of the field.

"He said to let you know he'd pick you and the *kinner* up tomorrow morning at ten o'clock." When Fern only nodded in response, Walker continued, "I want to get to the phone shanty as soon as possible to call my *mamm*, so I'm going to go round up Jane now."

Fern clapped the glass down, twirled around and blurted out, "Was Gloria with child before you married her?"

"Wh-what? Who told you that?" Walker didn't look nearly as appalled as Fern expected him to look. It must not have been the first time he'd heard the rumor.

"Stephen said Jane was too big to be premature. Was Gloria with child before you married her?" she repeated. The Amish rarely used the word *pregnant*, but even saying "with child" seemed immodest to Fern, given the context of what she was asking.

"Stephen doesn't know what he's talking about," Walker replied scornfully. But that wasn't the same as saying no.

Fern enunciated deliberately, replying, "I asked you a direct question. For the third time, was Gloria with child before you married her?"

"It's not what you think, Fern." Walker's mustache quivered as he replied. Oh, how Fern loathed the sight of that mustache now.

"You're right—it's *not* what I think. I never would have thought you'd do such a thing. *Neh*, stupid me, I actually started to believe you'd married Gloria because you were so distraught over Jordan's death that you weren't in your right mind! For the life of me, I couldn't comprehend any other reason for it! And now I know. But what I don't understand—what I'll *never* understand—is why you acted as if you loved me. If you and Gloria wanted to... to *court*, why did you claim your abiding love for me? Why would you deliberately trample on my heart like that? It was just plain *cruel.*"

"Ha!" Walker sneered. "Quit acting so wounded, Fern. Because for someone who claimed she'd never loved anyone the way she loved me, you sure got over me pretty fast. It took what, a couple of months for you to marry Marshall? I wanted you to marry me when we were nineteen and you made me wait for two more years. But you didn't even wait six more months until *hochzich* season to marry him."

"How dare you talk to me about waiting! You and Gloria didn't even wait until your wedding—" Fern stopped short, unable to complete the thought. She shoved past Walker and went into the living room, yanked one of the paper gifts from the twine around the staircase and returned to hold it up in front of his face. "You want to know why I married Marshall so quickly? *This* is why. Because I was so destitute I couldn't even afford to give anyone a *paper Grischtdaag* present!"

"So you married him for his money?" Walker shot back at her. "At least I married Gloria for a noble reason!"

"Noble? There was nothing noble about what the two of you did. You *had* to marry Gloria!" Fern couldn't stand to look at Walker. She turned her back toward him and peered out the window again. Gripping the edge of the sink, she said, "You can send Jane in to collect her things and say goodbye, but you are not *wilkom* to cross that threshold as long as I'm in this *haus*."

"You don't have to worry about that!" Walker barked. A few seconds later the door slammed behind him.

Fern worried she was about to be sick, but she fought the feeling and managed to catch her breath again before Jane came in. *"Daed* says we have to leave now."

"Jah." Fern couldn't say anything else without weeping and she didn't want Jane's last memory of her to be a sad one.

"I'm going to leave my card game upstairs for Phillip and Patience to keep and my chocolates for you. But I can't forget my presents." Jane plucked the papers from the twine then hugged Fern so hard her stomach hurt. "I love you," the little girl said, which made Fern's stomach hurt even more.

"I love you, too."

By the time Patience and Phillip came in, Fern had hung her coat up and washed her face, but Patience still noticed something was amiss. "Don't be sad, *Mamm. Gott* might still let us live in this *haus* and then we'll be able to see Jane and Walker again."

Neh, *I'm quite certain the Lord doesn't want us to live in this* haus. *And neither do I,* Fern thought. She couldn't fathom the idea of living anywhere near Walker now. It was one thing if he'd married Gloria because he'd been suffering from some kind of emotional upheaval after the accident. But to behave as he and Gloria had behaved? Fern saw no way to justify that, especially since he'd made a commitment to God and to the Amish way of life. Even more importantly, he'd never repented; if he had, he would have confessed his wrongdoing to the church and they would have accepted his apology. But Stephen made it clear no such thing had happened.

For the rest of the afternoon and into the evening, Fern seethed about how Walker acted as if *she'd* done something wrong by marrying Marshall! She was so upset she could hardly eat supper, and she was glad when the children didn't ask her to light the candles or sing carols, as she was in no mood for festivity. "Let's all go to bed early tonight, since the *Sabbat* is a day of rest," she suggested. "Tomorrow we'll celebrate with Jaala's *familye* and you'll need lots of energy since her *grooskinner* will probably want to build a snowman with you."

She tucked Patience in first. No sooner had the girl rested her head against the pillow than she popped upright again.

"*Mamm*, Jane forgot her dress and took yours instead!" Fern realized her daughter was right; after the accident she'd hung Jane's dress in the basement to dry and Jane had been wearing Fern's dress—with a pinned-up hem—for the past two days. She wished one of them would have thought of this sooner, especially since Fern only owned three dresses instead of four, as was customary. "Can we bring it to her?"

"*Neh*, we'll leave it here and her *groossmammi* can pick it up when they get home from Unity," Fern answered.

When she walked into Phillip's room, she stubbed her foot on something. Peeling back the small braided rug, she noticed one of the boards was off center. "What happened to the floor?"

"That's where we found the teacups. I couldn't make the board fit again."

Fern lifted up the plank, telling him he'd put it back upside down. When she did, she saw a dusty, leather-covered book in the little open compartment beneath it. She reached in and pulled it out. It must have been Gloria's journal. *It probably contains a lot of other secrets she literally swept under the carpet*, she thought bitingly and carried the diary downstairs.

Fern had no interest in perusing it, nor did she want anyone else to read it, so she opened it to tear out the pages for burning in the woodstove. Her eye caught on the phrase, "I don't want to marry Walker and I certainly don't love him."

It made Fern furious that her cousin hadn't even *wanted* to marry the man Fern had loved with her whole heart. She read on:

He doesn't love me, either. He said the only way he'd marry me is if we live as brother and sister, not as husband and wife. For the sake of the baby, we've also agreed to never, ever tell another soul why we got married.

I don't understand... Fern flipped back several pages to read, "If my father ever finds out I'm with child and the father was an *Englischer*, I don't know what he'll do."

Gasping, Fern collapsed onto the sofa. Jane's father was an *Englischer*? Then why did Walker marry Gloria? Fern turned back further in the journal until she found her answer. "I can't believe Jordan is gone. I am so scared. So alone."

Jordan. Jordan was Jane's daed*!* Fern scanned the diary greedily, unable to take in the information quickly enough. According to what her cousin had written, Gloria had been planning to leave the Amish in order to marry Jordan, even before she realized she was pregnant. Fern gathered that she was devastated by Jordan's sudden death and terrified Roman would send her out of his home if he found out. Knowing she couldn't make it on her own in the *Englisch* world, Gloria had confessed her dilemma to Walker on the day of Jordan's funeral.

"When I told Walker, I never expected him to say we should get married," Gloria had scrawled. Some of the ink was smeared across the page. "But he insists he can't allow the baby to grow up fatherless and homeless, not after Jordan gave his life to save Walker's. If I could think of any other way to help my baby without hurting Fern, I would do it..."

Fern dropped the book to the floor and pressed the heel of her hand against her mouth to keep the sobs from escaping her lips and waking the children. As she rocked back and forth, reflecting on Gloria's predicament and Walker's sacrifice, Fern cried and cried.

In retrospect, so many things he'd said to her since she returned to Serenity Ridge took on a new meaning. Like when he'd insisted, "I wouldn't tell you something unless I meant it." *He was referring to the past. He was saying he hadn't lied, that I really* was *the only woman he ever wanted for a wife.* Similarly, it had seemed so hypocritical that he'd been angry at her for marrying Marshall after he'd married Gloria first, but now Fern understood. She nearly wept herself sick, thinking about it.

By the time the sun came up, she hadn't been to bed at all. Fern climbed the stairs, declaring, *"Frehlicher Grischtdaag,"* in a loud voice.

Phillip was the first to rouse. *"Frehlicher Grischtdaag,"* he said. "Is it time to open our presents?"

Fern was confused. "I left your presents in Ohio, remember?"

"I mean the presents we made for each other downstairs."

"Oh, *jah*, we can open those. But instead of opening them now, I have a better idea."

"What is it, *Mamm*?" Patience asked from the hall.

Fern explained how it's always more fun to watch someone open a present you give them in person, so she suggested they ought to visit Jane and Walker at their house. "We can bring Jane's dress back, too. But it's a very long walk. Do you think you can make it?"

"Jah!" they cried together.

"Then let's hurry. We need to get there before they leave for their *ant* Willa's *haus*."

Within a few minutes, they'd set out. Frosted in white, tall pines glistened with touches of sunshine along both sides of the quiet country road. "Isn't this the perfect *Grischtdaag*?" Phillip asked Patience. The two of them skipped hand-in-hand in front of Fern until a buggy crested the hill in their direction and Fern urged them to move to the side of the street so it could safely pass.

But the buggy slowed to a stop and a man got out. *"Frehlicher Grischtdaag!"* he shouted, and it took a moment for Fern to recognize it was Stephen. She repeated the greeting and tried to walk around him but he blocked her way. "Can I speak with you a second?"

Since Fern had a word or two to get off her chest, as well, she told the children to wait by Stephen's buggy at the side of the road. Fern couldn't honestly defend Gloria, but she figured she could at least tell Stephen he was wrong about Walker, without betraying any confidences.

But before she could speak her piece, Stephen apologized. "I'm very sorry I said what I said about Walker yesterday. You were right. It wasn't gentlemanly. Nor was it fair of me to make assumptions or spread rumors."

Hearing the sincere penitence in his voice, Fern replied, "It's okay. I've been guilty of doing the same thing. Let's not mention it again, agreed?"

"Agreed." For some reason, Stephen wasn't wearing gloves, and he rubbed his hands together and then blew on his fingers. "What are you doing out walking so early this morning?"

When she told him she was returning Jane's dress before they left, Stephen offered to take Fern and the children to Walker's house.

"That would be *wunderbaar*. But weren't you going somewhere in the opposite direction?"

"*Jah*. I was going to apologize to you," he admitted sheepishly. "I didn't want you to leave Serenity Ridge without reconciling."

Gott *willing, I won't be leaving*, Fern thought. "I can't think of a better way to celebrate *Grischtdaag* than reconciling with a friend," she said.

Since the previous day was the Sabbath and unnecessary work was prohibited, Walker hadn't cleared his driveway. But this morning he funneled all of his anger at Fern into shoveling snow. *I could understand why Stephen Hertig would think Gloria and I had to get married, but Fern knows me better than to ask me a question like that! I courted her for almost three years—she knows that's not what I was like!*

Of course, it wasn't lost on Walker that he hadn't been able to deny that Gloria was with child when he married her, but he considered that to be beside the point. In his mind, Fern never should have questioned him in the first place. As for her reason for marrying Marshall so quickly? Walker didn't believe it for a second. If she had been that impoverished, she could have found a relative to live with. She could have gone to the church and asked for help. No, she was just making excuses. Making herself look like the injured party. She was so self-righteous...

Completely absorbed by his thoughts, Walker didn't notice that a buggy had pulled up in front of his house until the front door opened and Jane hollered, *"Frehlicher Grischtdaag!"* from the porch.

Of all people, it was Stephen who got out of the carriage, along with *Fern*. Then Patience and Phillip spilled out, too. *What's this about?* Walker jammed his shovel upright in the snow and turned to go check on Daisy in the stable. He had nothing to say to Fern and even less than nothing to say to Stephen.

But he couldn't ignore Phillip and Patience, who tore up the driveway, yelling that they'd brought Jane's dress back and they'd come to open their paper gifts with her. She held the door open and the three of them disappeared into the house before Walker could protest. Stephen waved before getting into his buggy and pulling away.

As Fern slowly approached him, Walker picked up the shovel again and started flinging snow to the side of the driveway. "You should have told Stephen to wait for the *kinner* to finish opening their gifts together." *Because I'm not giving you a ride.*

"That's okay. We can walk to Jaala's *haus* from here," Fern said. She stood off to his right and he nearly tossed a heap of snow onto her boots by accident.

"Could you move out of the way, please?"

"*Neh*. Could you stop shoveling, please?" When he didn't stop, Fern insisted, "Walker, I have something important to tell you and I don't want to have to shout."

If Fern was going to say something else about Gloria or Jane, Walker didn't want to hear it. But neither did he want the children to hear it, so he chucked one last scoopful of snow. "Make it quick," he allowed, but instead of giving her his full attention, he surveyed the driveway, trying to figure out how long it would take him to complete his task.

"I—I found a journal of Gloria's," she confessed. "I know about... Jordan and Jane. I know you and Gloria were never..."

Walker couldn't bear to talk about this subject. He winced and said, "That was a long time ago. It doesn't matter now."

"*Jah*, it does." Fern sidled closer. "It matters to me. It matters a *lot* to me."

Walker guffawed, unable to look at her, even though she was standing inches from him, for once not folding into herself but forcing herself into his space. She continued to speak. "You said I got over you quickly, but you're wrong. I've *never* gotten over you. I never loved Marshall the way I loved you."

"You married him." He squinted down at her. "You had two *kinner* with him."

"*Jah*, and I'll never say I regret having Phillip and Patience. Just like I know you'll never say you regret being Jane's *daed*," she countered, and she was right, but that didn't make Walker feel any better. "Even if you married Gloria for what you thought were very *gut* reasons, it still broke my heart, but I forgive you. Please, forgive me for breaking yours."

Walker wouldn't budge. After a few seconds of his stony silence, Fern said, "You were traumatized when you married Gloria, Walker. I married Marshall because I'd been traumatized, too. It was to a much lesser extent than when Jordan died, but when you married Gloria instead of me…" Fern swiped at her cheek. "I felt as if *you'd* died a sudden and unexpected death. And I did something desperate in response, just like you did. I didn't trust the Lord with my future—I didn't even ask Him what to do. I should have, but I didn't."

Every word Fern spoke resonated with truth, but Walker couldn't allow himself to believe she loved him. He glanced down the street. The van would arrive soon and he needed to change his clothes.

Apparently, Fern had more to say. "I want to stay in Maine. I want to live here for *gut*. But I can't if my living here is going to upset you. But whether I live here or in Ohio or anywhere else, you should know that I'll never stop loving you."

"But not the way a wife loves a husband." The words tasted bilious as Walker spoke them.

"What?"

"Patience told Jane you said it was nonsense to think you could love me the way a wife loves a husband."

It took a moment but Walker could practically see recollection dawn across Fern's face. "Oh, that," she said, rolling her eyes, but Walker wasn't amused. Glowering, he lifted his shovel again, but Fern grabbed it from him with a fierceness he hadn't seen in her before now. "Patience is a *kind*, Walker. Earlier in the week she told me she wanted you to…to ask me to marry you. I was afraid she'd start saying the same thing to Jane or to you and I didn't want you to feel uncomfortable. I didn't want you to think *I* was suggesting we get married."

"No chance I'd ever think that," Walker muttered, pushing his hat farther down on his head.

Fern's lower lip trembled as she gazed

up at him, her eyes awash with tears. Without breaking eye contact, she pulled off her glove and removed a square of folded paper from her palm. "This is for you. And for what it matters, I wrote it before I found Gloria's journal," she said, pressing it against his chest so he had to take it. "I'll go get the *kinner* now."

As she walked toward the house, Walker unfolded the paper and read, "If I could give you anything in the world, I'd give you my heart, but I can't because it's already yours and only yours."

Walker let the shovel clatter against the pavement. Charging toward Fern, he called her name. She had just reached the second porch step and she turned toward him, so that her beautiful silver eyes were level with his. He took hold of her hands and pulled her forward. After a long kiss, he murmured, "*Denki* for my *Grischtdaag* gift. It's exactly what I've always wanted."

Epilogue

"I'm *hallich Gott* let us live in *Onkel* Roman's *haus* for a whole year," Patience said as she climbed into the back of the buggy with Phillip and Jane. "But I'm *hallich* we got to move into a new *haus*, too."

Before marrying Fern, Walker had built a house for their family, with the help of the men in the district. Fern had told him she didn't need a new house, but Walker insisted on fulfilling the promise he'd made to her the first time he'd asked her to marry him.

"I'm *hallich* I get to have your *daed* for my second *daed*," Phillip announced.

"And I'm *hallich* I get to have your *mamm* for my second *mamm*," Jane copied.

Sitting in the front of the buggy, Walker and Fern exchanged glances. They'd talked about allowing Jane to read some of Gloria's diary once she was a little older so she could learn about Jordan. Walker still wasn't convinced this wasn't a violation of the agreement he'd made with Gloria, but Fern trusted that if they prayed about it first, God would help them make a wise decision.

As soon as they pulled out of the parking lot of Foster's Creamery after their second annual pre-Christmas treat, Fern shivered.

"Are you still cold from eating an ice cream cone?" Walker asked.

"*Jah.* A little bit."

He brought the horse to a halt so he could spread a blanket over Fern's lap. "Warm enough?" he asked.

"Not yet."

He unfolded a second blanket over her

legs and inched closer. "*Now* are you warm enough?"

"*Neh*, not yet," she replied, so he slid close enough to wrap his arm around her from the side and she snuggled against him. "There. *Now* I'm warm enough."

Now I'm home.

* * * * *

Don't miss any of these previous books in Carrie Lighte's Amish of Serenity Ridge miniseries:

Courting the Amish Nanny
The Amish Nurse's Suitor
Her Amish Suitor's Secret

And look for her novella in an Amish 2-in-1 anthology coming January 2021, only from Love Inspired!

Dear Reader,

I always enjoy researching Amish traditions (and recipes, eh-hem) and I was especially excited to discover that in many Amish communities the school's annual Christmas program is the most highly anticipated event of the academic year.

As a child, I loved participating in Christmas concerts at school and Christmas programs at church, so it was easy for me to imagine Jane's excitement and nervousness about reciting her verses in front of an audience. Like Jane, I also eagerly anticipated the special box of candy my Sunday school teacher gave us afterward.

I don't know if I'd feel as enthusiastic about performing onstage as an adult as I did when I was young, but I still love singing carols and reading the nativity story aloud with my family as a cherished part of our Christmas worship and celebration together.

However you're celebrating this year, I hope your Christmas is meaningful, merry, love-filled and bright.

Blessings,
Carrie Lighte